* *

The Bracelet

* *

Betsy Johnson-Miller

NORTH STAR PRESS OF ST. CLOUD, INC.
St. Cloud, Minnesota

Art by Mary Bruno

ISBN: 0-87839-322-6
ISBN-13: 978-0-87839-322-0

First Edition, May 1, 2009

Printed in the United States of America

Published by
North Star Press of St. Cloud, Inc.
P.O. Box 451
St. Cloud, Minnesota 56302

www.northstarpress.com

for Ben and Elise—
an adventure
like the one I always wished for

The Bracelet

* *

Prologue

S HE OPENED THE BOX. On a swirl of red velvet lay a bracelet made of the palest silver she had ever seen. One thin strand looped around and back, over and under, and in the center of its jumbled beauty rested a stone. "The moon," the girl whispered before she could stop herself. But it was more than that. Examining the stone closely, she saw it resembled all things of the sky: the moon, clouds, light, even air.

She tucked behind her ear a strand of brown hair that curled a little wildly around her face and wanted nothing more than to put the bracelet on her wrist, but she decided she'd better not. As if she were holding an egg, she gently placed the bracelet back in the box. And as she did this, she noticed it felt cold, almost dead, and heavier than it had earlier, and she had the craziest feeling that the bracelet was angry, or disappointed.

She took the box to the man sitting behind the green folding table. "How much do you want for this?"

"Five dollars."

It was all she had. "I'll take it."

When she got home, she ran upstairs to her bedroom and closed the door. Putting the box down on the bed next to her cat, she opened it and stared at the bracelet. Only then did she notice something sticking out of the velvet on top. It looked like a bit of the backing had come loose. She picked at it with a fingernail. It moved. It was loose. A gentle tug and a piece of paper came free. Unfolding it, she read:

Dear Child, (You have no idea how odd this is, but you will someday.) This bracelet has been in our family for generations; every girl receives it when she is sixteen. If you choose to wear the bracelet, you must leave it on. Oh, yes, and remember to open your heart and believe.

Lena Way

* 1 *

Leaving

WHAT DOES ONE PACK for *an adventure?*" fourteen-year-old Litney Way asked, her fingers drumming on the top of the suitcase.

"Your sarcasm is noted and ignored," her mother answered, rolling a pair of thick socks and stuffing them in her duffel bag. "Look, if you don't want to do this, put the bracelet back in the box."

"What, and not save the world?" Litney said as she put a sweater in the yellow suitcase with big red flowers on the inside lining.

The suitcase had been under the stairs at her grandparents for years. She used to sneak in the slanted closet when she thought the adults weren't looking. She would open the suitcase and sit inside it. Somehow she had known it was meant for traveling, and she'd sit there, her mind taking her high in the sky or careening down a river. When she turned seven, when she quit doing things like that because it was something babies did, her grandmother had given her the suitcase, saying, "You never know when you'll need this." There had been a strange look in her grand-mother's eyes as she said that. Now Litney couldn't help but wonder if that had something to do with this.

Lena Way stilled her daughter's hand, which had begun drumming again. "I'm serious. If you don't want to—"

Litney shrugged her mother's hand away. "Excuse me if I think this is a little weird. I bring a bracelet home from a garage sale, and inside its box, I find a note from *my mother.*"

"It was a nice note, if I do say so myself," her mother said with a smug smile.

"That's not the point," Litney said, irritated. "The point is I want to know why you aren't freaked out by this. Adults are never supposed to believe this stuff."

"What was the last thing my note told you?" Lena asked her daughter, her tone now just a bit haughty.

It took Litney a moment to remember. "Believe. But believe what?" she wanted to know.

With another little smile, her mother said, "You'll know when it's time."

"But both you and the note said it wasn't time," Litney answered. "Why is it here now?"

Her mother's face grew serious. "I don't know. The bracelet is supposed to appear to all the women in our family when they turn sixteen. Not fourteen. It must be something serious."

Litney said, "Can you tell me again why we have to go to Grandma's and Pop's?"

"Because that is where it happens."

"Where what happens?" Litney demanded.

Lena looked at her daughter as she zipped up her bag and slung it over her shoulder. "We've been through this."

"So, you're really not going to tell me? You're going to make me go into this blind?"

It was an accusation, like the barb Litney had thrown at her mother earlier that morning about not feeling as important as her parents' careers. Litney sensed that her mother wanted nothing more than to tell her everything, to explain how that bracelet had changed her own life, maybe, but she knew she could not. She'd said it was forbidden. "It's for the best. It's different for everyone."

"Can you at least tell me what it was like for you?" Litney asked.

"It changed me." There was something in her mother's face that made Litney stare. A softening. "It showed me nothing's impossible. It brought me your father. It made me who I am. That's all I can say. Are you ready?"

"What do you mean it brought you Dad? How could it do that? You were sixteen? You weren't married at sixteen."

Her mother didn't answer.

"Mom?" When Litney realized her mother wasn't going to tell her anything else, she said, "Fine. Let's go."

THE THREE-HOUR RIDE to her grandparents' farm was silent except for the thrum of the wheels on the road. Both Litney and her mother seemed content to nurse their own thoughts. Lena kept chewing on her lip. Litney watched her mother out of the corner of her eye and wondered if her mother was thinking about how Litney had said she never saw her parents anymore because all they did was work. Litney knew she was right, and she knew this would bother her mother. Both Lena and Litney's father, Joe, had to travel a lot for their work to save endangered species, and that often meant journeying halfway around the globe. In fact, at this moment, Litney's father was on the island of Madagascar trying to save the black lemur from extinction. Her parents had sat her down many times to justify how they could leave their only child so often, telling her their work was "vital," "important," "life or death." Litney understood that—it's not like she hated animals or wanted to see the different species gone. It just didn't help her miss her parents any less. She had a hard time remembering the last time the three of them had done something together as a family. Since Litney had finally been able to tell her mother how much she hated them being gone all the time, perhaps her parents would reconsider what they were doing.

Who was she kidding? Her opinions and feelings never mattered at all to them before this. That's why Litney hated the bracelet, why she wanted to throw the bracelet out the window as she and her mother drove north to her grandparents' farm. She didn't want to have anything to do with the bracelet. How she had gotten it with her own mother's message inside was creepy, to say the least. More than that, she wanted to get rid of the bracelet because it was obviously so important to her mother that she keep it and wear it. Even this was all about her mother and what she wanted. Her mother didn't care what was important to Litney—it felt like no one did.

She wished her father were here—he would have seen how bizarre this was. He at least would have forced her mother to stop and explain everything. He would have said, "Let's hold on a minute and figure all of this out." But he wasn't here, and Litney felt very alone as she and her mother drove north into the oncoming night.

"WE'RE HERE."

Her mother's soft voice roused Litney. "Hmm? Oh." As she rubbed her eyes, she heard a screen door slap wood. Her grandmother hurried out of the big old farmhouse.

"So, it's happened?" Lily Way's voice was excited as she hugged her daughter. Litney was busy getting her face washed by Bernard, her grandparents' mammoth St. Bernard.

"She found it at a garage sale this morning," Litney's mother answered.

"It's early, isn't it?" Her grandmother's voice quieted and sounded worried.

"It must be something urgent," her mother replied just as softly.

"You don't have to talk about me like I'm a moron," Litney grumbled, rubbing the dog's thick scruff.

"Oh, dearie," her grandmother said, hugging her stiff granddaughter tightly. "I'm so excited for you, although . . ."

"Although what?" Litney wanted to know.

"Nothing, nothing. Why don't you come inside? Pop's anxious to see you."

"Can he tell me anything about what's going on?" Litney asked, not very hopeful since it seemed like everyone wanted to keep her in the dark about this.

"I'm afraid he doesn't know much more than you. It's the women, you see." Her grandmother paused and giggled. "As it should be."

Her grandfather came out onto the porch. "Litney Girl. Come here."

And Litney went. In her grandfather's arms, she felt all her concerns and anger melt away. This was the one thing that was always sure in her life. No matter how horrible she was feeling, whenever she saw her Pop, she knew everything would be all right.

"They tell me it's happened," he whispered into her hair.

Litney pulled back. "But I don't know what 'it' is."

Her grandfather kissed the top of her head, then asked, "Does it matter? Let's go into the kitchen. I'll fix you one of my famous apple butter sandwiches."

As Litney ate her sandwich with Bernard waiting expectantly at her feet, she marveled, as she always did, at her grandparents' farm. They made everything they needed to live—just like the pioneers had. In fact, the entire sandwich she was noisily chewing had been grown and produced on the farm. The bread, the apples. But what was more odd was that people came from miles around to visit "Plain and Simple," as their farm was called. Not only did folks visit—they usually came to stay and work for a week or two, and they *paid* her grandparents to do it. "When you want it plain and simple," was the farm's motto, and, obviously, that was something people wanted. The only two weeks when they weren't booked with visitors were Thanksgiving and Christmas. Otherwise, the two smaller barns that had been converted into bunkhouses were always full.

"It's early," Pop said as he plunked down a glass of fresh milk in front of her. That, too, came from the farm.

"That's what everyone keeps saying, but what does it mean?" She slipped the dog a piece of her crust.

Her grandfather stared at his large calloused hands that lay clasped on the table. "Don't know, but then I don't know much about the whole thing.

6

All's I know is it was that bracelet that gave your grandmother the idea to start this here farm and your mother the idea to work to save endangered animals."

"What if I don't want to do what it wants me to do?" Litney asked.

"Then don't."

The blue-faced clock above the sink made the only sound in the room. *Tick, tick, tick.* "I'm scared," Litney admitted.

"I would be, too." He covered his granddaughter's small hands in his own big, warm hands. "But it seems to me that bracelet did right by your grandmother and mother. Don't see any reason it wouldn't do the same for you."

She felt Pop's thumb touch the bracelet. "Can I see it?" he asked. "I've heard so much about it, but I never got a chance to see it when your mother had it. I was away helping a friend raise a barn."

Litney held out her wrist, and her grandfather turned it this way and that to examine the fine craftsmanship of the piece.

"It's growing warm," she told him.

Her grandfather's eyes widened. "Well, I never . . ."

She laughed. "If I didn't know better, I would think you never believed Grandma."

Leaning forward, he whispered, "I don't think I did. Not really and completely. Until now."

AN HOUR LATER, her mother opened the door to Litney's bedroom and told her to try to get some sleep. "You're going to need it."

Litney thought about telling her there was no way she was going to sleep tonight—too much had happened today. But as soon as her mother closed the door, she felt her eyelids grow heavy. The bracelet was still warm, and it soothed her. Had she been awake enough, she would have thought it was actually slowing her pulse down, down, down.

She slept.

7

2

Dokken

S HE DIDN'T KNOW WHAT had awakened her—a noise, Bernard kicking her as he slept beside her, or the bracelet. It had grown uncomfortably warm, and Litney thought about removing it until she remembered her mother's note. She had to leave the bracelet on. Out the window, the first streaks of dawn stained the dark sky. The clock on her bedside table said it was only a little after five, but somehow, Litney knew she wouldn't be able to fall back asleep.

After a yawn and a body-shaking stretch, she got dressed. "Come on, boy," she whispered to the dog. Not that it mattered how quiet she was. The whole house trembled when Bernard jumped off the bed.

They went downstairs. Litney made herself bread with blackberry jam, then headed out into the gray dawn. She walked on past the two small barns where the visitors slept, on past the big barn, out to her favorite spot in the whole world—the atrium. It was set at the edge of a copse of trees and looked like a huge bird cage covered in ivy, the metal buried in a soft quiet green.

Litney told Bernard to stay. While there was more than enough room inside for the two of them, she knew he would only noisily pant and scratch, and what she craved right now more than anything was silence.

The entry to the atrium was low, and Litney had to stoop to crawl through it. Inside, she immediately took a deep breath and exhaled. Small red roses hid among the ivy, and the fragrance soothed her. The floor was bare dirt, but this was the only place in the world where Litney didn't mind getting dirty. She lay on her back in the middle of the atrium and looked out the small hole in the top that her grandfather kept meticulously trimmed. The sky above was pink now, and everything was still—except for the birds. They had gotten downright noisy, carrying on so that they almost sounded like her gossipy classmates at school.

"Trudy is lazy," Litney heard one bird say in a loud voice. "Those babes of hers are gonna starve."

"Don't I know it," another replied, this one's voice much more pleasant. "Why I dropped off a couple of worms just yesterday for them, I felt so sorry."

Litney's eyes were closed, and she smiled. It was no wonder she never got up at this time of the day. She was so tired, she was imagining birds could talk.

"Would you look? Do you see what I see?"

"The bracelet."

Litney's eyes flashed open, and she saw two dark shadows sitting up in the opening of the atrium above her.

"But it's early," the loud one whispered.

"I wish everyone would quit saying that," Litney said, and then she realized what she had done. She had spoken to a bird. Closing her eyes again, she shook her head. "I must be tired. Talking to a dumb bird."

One of the shadows circled down, landed beside her and glared at her with daring black eyes. "Who are you calling dumb?"

Litney sat up and scuttled crab-like to the edge of the atrium wall. "You . . . you . . . you didn't just speak. There's no way. You didn't speak to me. You couldn't have."

"Then who did?" the bird asked, hopping toward her.

Litney's laugh was edgy. "This is ridiculous. Birds don't talk."

"What about parrots?" came the reasonable reply.

"They only repeat words. They repeat what they have heard someone else say," Litney protested. "They don't know what the words mean. Don't know what they're saying."

"You realize you're now arguing with a bird," the pleasant one pointed out as she fluttered down beside the girl.

Litney opened her mouth, but before she could respond, she heard a noise at the entrance of the atrium. Bernard whined. The startled birds flapped up toward the opening, and Litney saw a bright red head poking its way inside.

Startled blue eyes fixed on her. "Who are you?" asked a bewildered boy about her age in a rumpled t-shirt and shorts. He had so many freckles in shades of tan, beige, and brown that his skin looked orange.

Embarrassed about being caught in such peculiar behavior and afraid he had heard her talking to the birds, Litney didn't answer. Instead she demanded, "Who are you and what are you doing here?"

He blinked. His face reddened. "Dokken."

"What?" she asked, thinking he must be speaking a foreign language.

"My name. Dokken."

"What sort of name is that?" she asked.

He sighed. "My parents wanted something different," the boy explained as he stood up and walked slowly around the perimeter of the atrium, looking all around. "What sort of place is this? I've never seen any-thing like it."

"It's an atrium, and for your information," she retorted haughtily, "my grandparents own this place. And because they do, I belong here and you don't. So, I am going to ask you to go back to . . . to wherever it is you came from. I need to do some thinking. Here. Alone."

The boy, who was wearing two shoes but only one sock, picked a rose off one of the vines and smelled it. "That's gonna be pretty hard," he said.

"And why is that? You have two feet and there's the door."

He looked, then turned back to her. "But . . . where am I?"

Litney, still irritated, now began to grow worried. Was this kid sick in the head? How could he not know where he was? "What do you mean where are you?"

He shrugged. "I don't know where I am. But you seem to have a good fix on where you are, so I thought it made sense to ask you to shed some light on the situation."

"How can you not know where you are?" Litney asked, planting her fists on her hips. "Are you crazy?"

He almost laughed. "Normally, I'd say no, but at this moment I'm not entirely sure. All I know is I was sleeping in my bed, and then suddenly I woke up and . . . I was here."

"Do you always sleep in clothes and shoes?" she asked pointing to his rumpled clothes.

He looked down at himself, twisting the foot with no sock. "We spent the day at an outdoor concert and didn't get home till late. I was really tired. I think I just sort of fell into bed."

This was making no sense and the boy wasn't helping one bit. Litney thought carefully. "Where is your bed?" she asked.

"In our apartment," Dokken answered.

Litney let out a long breath. "And where is that?" She was getting more and more annoyed at this boy.

"New York City."

She felt a little chill climb her spine. Then she thought he must be lying. "That's absurd," she said.

"Having an apartment in New York City is *not* absurd," the boy replied very calmly and reasonably. "Nearly everyone who lives in New York City has an apartment."

Litney stared at this boy who obviously loved to argue. If what this weird orange-faced, red-haired kid said was true, this situation was bizarre, but instead of being worried, for the moment he seemed to be having fun.

"No. I certainly didn't mean it was absurd that you live in an apartment or even that that apartment is in New York. What I do mean is that this is Minnesota. It's absurd to believe you can go to bed in a New York City apartment and wake up in Minnesota."

"Not unless my folks hopped on a plane with me," Dokken said and smiled. "Or I was abducted by aliens. Are you an alien?"

Litney's eyes narrowed. She was not amused. "So your folks arrived here last night at my grandparents' farm to work, right?"

Dokken gave a weak smile. "Look. I went to sleep in my own bed last night. The one in New York. I woke up in my own bed . . . under the covers. I'm absolutely sure of that. It's when I poked my head out of the covers that I was here."

She stared, then asked the boy nearly the same question she had asked her mother yesterday. "How come you aren't freaking out?"

Dokken gave that a moment's thought, then shrugged. "Losing it right now wouldn't really help the situation, now would it?"

"Probably not," Litney had to agree, "but that wouldn't stop me."

The two of them looked at each other for a bit. Finally, Litney couldn't stand it any longer. "Hey, I know this is weird, but could you leave me alone? I need to think, and I'm asking nicely. Please."

He eyed the entry of the atrium and shook his head. "I don't what would happen." He plopped down on the ground and looked out the hole as she had done earlier.

This was one more instance of how out of control Litney felt lately. Her father was gone and who knew how long it would be before he came back. Her mother was home at the moment but continually working, and there was nothing she could do about that either. Now the whole mysterious bracelet thing and the talking birds and this stupid boy who had suddenly appeared out of nowhere and thought he'd come from New York City. It was more than she could take. "Get out!" she yelled, actually stamping her foot.

"And they say redheads have tempers," the boy smirked. He leaned toward her, "I don't want to leave. I think I'll stay here all day."

Losing complete control, Litney shouted, "You're a freak! A freaky looking boy with a freaky sounding name. Freak! Freak!"

Blood infused the boy's face, turning it deep magenta. Even his freckles seem to fill with color. "I've been taunted and teased about my hair, my name, my freckles ever since kindergarten. I hate it! It's just not fair!" Dokken shoved Litney hard, and she fell backwards, banging her head against metal. While it was covered with ivy, a clang still echoed in the morning air.

"Awh," Litney groaned and put a hand to the back of her head. When she looked at it, her palm had a bright red streak of blood.

Immediately, Dokken knelt beside her. "I'm sorry. I'm really, really sorry. I shouldn't have done that. It's just . . . are you okay?"

Gingerly, she touched her head again. "Ouch. Yeah, I'll be fine. Anyway, it was my fault. I shouldn't have said what I said. It was mean."

Relieved that he hadn't killed her, Dokken slumped into a cross-legged position. He put a stick in the way of an ant and watched the ant crawl over it. "You're right though. I am a freak. So are my folks. Who names their child Dokken? Red heads both of them, and Dad has freckles just like mine. Except I got more freckles and redder hair." He grabbed a clump of hair on either side of his head. "This stupid hair . . ." his voice trailed off as he stared into space, deflating into an unhappy slump.

"My name isn't much better," Litney said, glad to see the blood was slowing. None came away the last time she'd touched the sore spot. "And Dokken is . . . interesting," she added rather lamely. "I mean, what fun would it be to be one of four Matts or the third Jessica? At least when my teacher says, 'Litney,' I know she means me. You've got that going for you, too."

"Uh huh," the boy's sarcasm was obvious.

It grew quiet between them. The sun was beginning its long climb in the sky, and suddenly managed to find a crack in the ivy. A ray caught the silver on Litney's wrist. "Hey, that's a cool bracelet," Dokken said.

Litney had forgotten all about it, but when she looked at her hand, she noticed her wrist felt tingly. The sensation wasn't painful, just odd. "Thanks." Not knowing how much else she could say, she remained silent.

Dokken seemed to come to a decision. He stood and brushed off his jeans. "Well, I'll leave you alone now. I'll go outside and . . ."

"And what?" Litney asked. "Start walking back to New York? You don't have to go." She was surprised she meant it.

"Yeah. Well, you are right. This is weird. I'd better go outside and see what I can do. See ya around." Dokken's red hair disappeared through the opening. Then she heard, "Uh, Litney. You'd better come out here."

14

* 3 *

The Hole

L ITNEY NOTICED THREE THINGS as she crawled out of the atrium. The first was that it was dark. Since it had been almost light when she arrived earlier, the thought occurred to her that it was either going to rain, or there was an eclipse no one had remembered to tell her about. The second thing was the smell—it was no longer the rosy scent of the atrium, or even the fresh smell of early morning in the country. Instead, her nose detected an odor that was strong and dusky. Finally, she wondered where Bernard had wandered off to. "Dokken?"

"Over here," he said, standing next to a shadowy hole.

It wasn't until that moment that Litney realized she wasn't outside. Rather she and Dokken were in a dirt room no bigger than her bedroom at home. All the walls were solid except for the hole near Dokken that was the size of the saucer sled she used to slide down hills in the winter. As Litney walked closer to him, she heard a noise that sounded like an animal scratching. "Is that Bernard?" she asked, feeling both confusion and concentration.

15

"Who's Bernard?"

"My grandparents' dog. He's a St. Bernard," Litney replied.

"No, I don't think it's Bernard." Dokken waited for the girl to have some reaction to the fact that the two of them were not standing outside the atrium where they should have been. When that didn't happen, he began to worry that the bump on Litney's head had done more damage than just the cut. "Litney?"

She cocked her head and looked at him.

"Do you see anything wrong?" Dokken asked.

"Well, it does smell a little." She crinkled her nose like a little child would.

"Besides that?" Dokken asked.

"We're in a dirt room," Litney said slowly.

"Yes."

Her eyebrows drew together. "We shouldn't be in a dirt room." She looked at him, and her eyes grew clear and bright. "We were in the atrium, and then you called me. I went through the door and came out in here. This isn't where we were supposed to come out."

Dokken could hear the panic building in her voice. Very soothingly, he said, "Don't worry. We'll figure this out."

Litney looked behind her and ran her hands over the dirt. The wall was solid. "Where's the door to the atrium? The door I just came through?"

"I don't know," he replied honestly, trying to ignore the fear taking hold of her eyes. He had to think. Both he and Litney had gotten out of the atrium by a door that no longer existed. They weren't outside like they should have been. They were in a room with no windows. "So, why isn't it completely dark?"

Litney looked around. If they were in a room with no windows, she realized she shouldn't have been able to see a thing. While it would have been difficult to read, she had no trouble seeing Dokken's face or the walls of the cave. She wondered where the light was coming from. She looked to the hole, but it was dark. Then she saw her bracelet. The stone glowed softly, like a candle. "Dokken, look."

He followed her finger to look at her wrist. "It's glowing. Cool," Dokken said.

"And it feels warm again. Maybe this is what they were all talking about," Litney mused aloud.

"What?" Dokken took a step closer.

"Oh." Litney thought about telling him nothing. After all, her mother and grandmother had kept everything a secret—even, it seemed, from her grandfather. But why would Dokken be here if he wasn't supposed to know what was going on? Taking a risk, she quickly told him what had happened the day before. "Mom drove me up to Grandma and Pop's as soon as we had finished packing. No one could tell me what was going to happen. They just kept saying it was an 'adventure.'"

Dokken nodded a few times. "Looks like the adventure's already begun."

"But . . . why are you here?" Litney asked pointedly. When she saw the hurt her question caused, she explained, "I thought this was supposed to happen to *me*. But I'm glad you're here. I'd be really scared right now if I was all alone."

That brightened his expression, which Litney was beginning to understand was particularly easy to read because of his redness. "What do we do now?" Dokken wanted to know.

"It doesn't look like we have much of a choice," she said, pointing to the hole. Litney hadn't lied—she liked to think of herself as brave, but she couldn't even begin to say how relieved she was to have this red-haired boy she had just met with her.

17

Dokken offered, "If you give me the bracelet for light, I'll go first."

She considered it, but then shook her head. She remembered her mother's warning. "My mother made it very clear I can't take it off, and that means I have to go first." Taking a deep breath, she climbed into the hole. Dokken followed.

They crawled along a tunnel for several minutes before Dokken said, "It feels like we are going down."

"I thought I noticed that, too," whispered Litney over her shoulder.

"Do you see anything yet?"

"No."

Like swimming in a lake, the two of them passed through pockets of warmth and coolness. The only noises they could hear were their own movements, their own breathing, and an occasional scratching. Since neither of them was wearing a watch, they couldn't tell how long they crawled through the tunnel. It could have been minutes or hours.

As they crawled, they were silent for the most part, and so Dokken's voice seemed especially loud when he said, "I smell something."

Litney stopped, and Dokken bumped into her. She laughed, "Sorry." Litney put her nose into the air. "Me, too. It smells like . . ."

"Roses," Dokken said.

"Yeah. Roses." She crawled more quickly now, noticing that the light in the tunnel was growing. Finally she hauled herself out of the tunnel and turned to offer Dokken a hand as he crawled out.

"I don't believe it," he said.

"I don't get it," Litney replied. "We're back in the atrium."

"The tunnel must have been some sort of a circle."

"Well, what's the point in that?" Litney was angry. It took her a moment to figure out why. Ever since she had found the bracelet, everyone had been preparing her for this grand adventure. Somewhere in that tunnel, it seemed she had finally gotten herself ready to do this, whatever this was, but now it seemed to be over before it had even started. She heard Dokken shuffling his feet behind her and turned. Feeling dumb now that she had told him they were going on an adventure, she shrugged and said, "Sorry."

The boy smiled. "I might have been a little afraid, but I thought it was going to be pretty cool."

Litney smiled as well. "Yeah, me, too."

"Now what do we do?" he asked.

"I guess we'd better head back to the farmhouse, get some breakfast and find out how to get you home."

Dokken followed her out into the morning—the actual morning this time—and the two of them talked as they walked. Dokken told her, "I don't have any brothers or sisters."

"Neither do I," Litney said.

"Don't you wish you did?" he asked.

"No, not really. You do?"

"Yeah," Dokken replied in a passionate whisper.

"Why? I think we have it perfect being only kids. No one to fight with, no one to annoy us, no one to take our stuff."

Dokken had stopped walking. He was staring at something. "It's beautiful," he said, pointing at a purple flower.

"That? That's a thistle. See the thorns on the green part? People around here hate them. They get in the fields and they're almost impossible to get rid of."

"But they're beautiful. Look at that color."

Litney looked at Dokken. It wasn't only that he was missing a sock, or that he had an odd name. There was something different about him. "Dokken, why do you want a brother or a sister?"

The boy shrugged. "We move a lot. My parents, well, they don't function real well in the real world. I guess neither do I. It'd be kinda nice to have someone else like me. Too late now, though, I suppose."

Litney couldn't think of a thing to say, except, "My parents, they work all the time."

"See?" Dokken said. "If you had a sibling that wouldn't matter."

"I suppose. Hey, there's Bernard." Litney whistled, and the huge dog cocked its head and came bounding toward her. When he got close, however, the dog skidded to a stop and began barking. "Bernard, come here, boy." The dog only barked harder. Bernard loved her—why was he doing this? Embarrassed this was happening in front of someone else, Litney took a step toward the dog. "Come on, boy. It's me." Bernard turned and ran ten feet away, whipping around to continue his wild barking.

Dokken asked, "Can I try?"

Litney hid her tears and said, "Yeah, sure."

"Bernard, hey buddy." He crept forward and clicked his tongue. "Come here."

This time Bernard dashed off entirely, hiding somewhere behind the house.

"I don't understand," Litney said, tears falling down her cheeks now. It had been a horrible morning. What else could go wrong?

Dokken suggested, "Let's go get some breakfast."

They approached the back door of the house. Bernard was nowhere to be seen as they climbed the steps.

While it was still early in the morning, the sun had gained strength, and both Litney and Dokken were glad to get in the cool dark of the house. They went into the oddly empty and silent kitchen where the clock on the wall said it was a little after eight.

20

Litney asked, "Where is everyone? Breakfast is served at eight." It had always been served at eight, for the family and any guests who might be staying at the farm.

Dokken shrugged.

"Maybe they are all in the dining room." Litney walked through the kitchen and pushed open the swinging door to the dining room. Before she had gotten half way through, however, she stepped back into the kitchen. Her face was pale.

"What?" Dokken asked.

"Something's not right."

Litney looked so shaken that Dokken pushed the door open slowly, half expecting to be attacked. He saw eight or ten people around a table, and their mouths were moving as if they were talking, but there was no sound. The room was absolutely silent. He went back into the kitchen. "I don't get it."

Without answering him, Litney pushed through the door and approached her mother. "Mom?" Litney tried to tap her mother on the shoulder. Her finger went all the way through her mother's body, like it was going through water. Litney's expression was horrified as she backed away and ran toward Dokken.

When the two of them were back in the kitchen, Dokken said, "I'm not sure how many times we can ask this, but what's going on?"

* 4 *

Grufwin

"WHAT'S GOING ON?" DOKKEN ASKED AGAIN, this time to Litney's back because she was heading out the screen door. "Hey, wait up!"

But Litney didn't. She even broke into a run—through the field of ankle-high corn, down the wooded gully and out to the pond. Only when she reached the water's edge did she drop to the ground.

"You're fast," Dokken huffed as he landed beside her. When he saw the way she was glaring at her bracelet, he asked, "Is it hurting you?"

"No. But it's stupid. It's just so stupid!"

"It seemed like you were kinda disappointed when you thought the adventure wasn't—"

"I was, and that's what's so stupid. Just when I think one thing, something else happens. And Bernard, and the breakfast table—what was that?" Litney picked up a flat rock and skimmed it across the surface of the pond, startling a blue heron into flight.

"Watch it!" they heard.

"Please tell me you said that," Litney whispered.

"No," Dokken replied, his eyes never wavering from the big bird as it landed right in front of them.

"Didn't you see me?" the heron asked.

"No, I didn't. I wouldn't have thrown the rock if I had," Litney answered. "I was upset."

With small glittering eyes, the heron seemed to be deciding if Litney was telling the truth or not.

"You see what you choose to see," the heron said.

"True, but you have to admit you also don't want to be seen," Litney argued. "Why else would you stand so still and blend into your environment so well?"

"Well said—you! You have the bracelet." The heron flapped his wings slightly, his small eyes glittering intently.

"Yes, I do, and if you say it's too early, I will kindly strangle that long thin neck of yours."

The heron laughed with a kind of *squawk*, or at least Litney assumed the noise was laughter. "All right, I won't say it if you promise not to throw any more rocks."

"Deal," Litney said just a fraction of a second ahead of Dokken's same agreement.

"I am Grufwin," the heron said.

"I'm Litney."

"Dokken."

"I have heard the legends about another who came with a bracelet. I wasn't alive then."

"That's probably my mother," Litney told him. "Or it could be my grandmother. They say all of the women in my family do this."

"Might I see the bracelet?"

Litney held out her arm, and the bird turned his head to the side, so his beak wouldn't peck her, and brought one eye close to her wrist. "It is as beautiful as the crickets say."

"What?" Dokken asked.

"The crickets—poets, bards, troubadours," Grufwin told them. "On summer nights, they sing to us of things past and things to come. Recently they've been singing of the one to come, telling us she would come very soon, but no one believed them. Like the rhythms of the earth, there's a timing to the coming of the one with the bracelet."

"That's why everyone keeps saying it's early," Dokken whispered.

"Exactly," Grufwin answered, even though Dokken hadn't spoken to him. "All creatures get used to things the way they are, and it's sometimes hard for them to accept the way things will be." His words sounded very adult, but his voice also sounded young and dreamy.

"You are very wise," Litney noted.

Grufwin pulled his beak to his right shoulder, a gesture of humility. "I thank you. Coming from the one who comes, that is a blessing."

Dokken asked, "How old you are? You seem old . . . but not, if that makes any sense."

"In your years, I am three. In heron years, I'm 153."

"You have different years than we do?" Dokken tried to clarify.

"In a way. What I mean is time is different for us."

"Time is time," Litney said. "You just must count differently."

"No," Grufwin said patiently, "time is different for us."

"But that can't be," Litney persisted.

"Why not?"

Litney thought, "Well, because time is time. It can't be different for different people."

24

"Why not?" Grufwin wanted to know.

Frustrated, Litney said, "I don't know. I'm not a scientist or anything. But time is time—"

"You've said that three times now," Grufwin said. "Repetition doesn't create truth."

Thinking maybe Litney was getting angry, and before a fight broke out, Dokken said, "What does it mean to be 153 years old in heron years?"

"It means I'm nearing adulthood."

"Oh. Does that mean you'll have a family soon?" Dokken asked.

"Soon," Grufwin said, "but first I must go to the Universe to study the laws."

"Don't you mean go to *university* to study law?" Litney couldn't help correcting him after the way he had challenged her.

Grufwin regarded her down his long bill. "Unlike humans, herons say what they mean," he said, and there was an edge to his voice. "I am going to the Universe to study the laws."

Dokken gave Litney a look, hoping to calm her down, clearly not comfortable with other people fighting. He turned his attention back to Grufwin and asked, "Okay. What does that mean?"

"It means the Universe will teach me what makes it work."

"Oh, you mean like the laws of gravity, relativity, all those sorts of scientific things?"

"Exactly. And if I do well at that, then I will go on to Outlaws."

"Outlaws?" Litney snapped. "Do they teach you to brandish pistols, wear hats and talk with a twang?"

"Litney!" Dokken whispered.

"Sorry," she muttered, not liking one bit the disappointed look Grufwin had about his face.

"Outlaws is where you learn about how all the laws can be broken, or that they never even existed in the first place."

"Like time," Dokken offered.

Litney didn't like the look of admiration that comment got Dokken.

"Yes. Like time, Dokken."

Litney stood and brushed off the seat of her pants. "It was great talking with you, Grufwin, but we need to get going."

"Where?" Dokken asked.

Grufwin fluffed out his feathers then settled them, and Litney could see that the heron was also curious to hear her answer.

She didn't know, so she said, "Everyone keeps saying this is an adventure, but I've never heard of an adventure where one sits around talking with a bird." Knowing how mean she sounded, she added, "It was wonderful to meet you, Grufwin. I hope you do well at Universe so you can make it into Outlaws."

"Thank you. Might I offer one suggestion?" Grufwin asked.

Litney wanted to tell him she didn't need any help or his wisdom, that she could figure everything out all on her own. But knowing that wasn't true, she sighed and nodded.

He told her, "Make your way to the big river to the West. Stay on this side of it until you come to the Rock that Boils."

"Why?" Litney wanted to know.

"An adventure spent talking with a bird might not be any good, but then neither is one where the heroine doesn't know what she's supposed to be doing."

Litney knew she should apologize. She knew she should say she was so worried about all of this that she wasn't herself. But she only raised a hand and waved. Then she turned and began walking.

"SHE'S SCARED," DOKKEN TOLD GRUFWIN in the silence left behind by the lack of an apology.

"She should be," Grufwin answered. "But she should also be present where she is present."

Dokken smiled. "You'll make it into Outlaws, no problem."

"Thank you. Now there's something I must say to you, but I'll be brief," Grufwin said, since Litney's figure was getting smaller and smaller. "You have your own task on this adventure. You know that, don't you?"

Dokken said, "I kinda figured that. Will I be told by someone what that is?"

"I think you already know," Grufwin answered.

"I have to take care of her?"

"She'll take care of herself. But you must do whatever it takes to allow her make it all the way through this adventure. Are you willing to do that? Because if you aren't, you can go back right now."

Dokken wasn't going to ask how, but he knew Grufwin spoke the truth. His mind flitted all over the place. He thought about his warm bed back in New York City, his mother's hands as she handed him a bowl of oatmeal, then the bathroom stall at school the bullies always chased him into. "I . . . I am willing."

"Then go."

Dokken wanted to make a parting gesture, but how does one hug a heron, or shake his wing? He bowed. Grufwin looked flattered and bowed back.

Then Dokken ran to catch up with Litney.

* 5 *

The Dogs

ONLY THE SOUND OF THE GRASS and wind was between them. Litney was angry with herself, and Dokken didn't know what he should say.

"Do you know where we are going?" he asked, sometime later, hope in the back of his voice. "Even though I've walked all over the city with my parents, this is different. There are hills . . . and sounds . . . and some darn bugs that keep zooming around my head, buzzing loudly in my ear and trying to crawl in my hair to bite me."

Litney glanced at him. "Last year, my grandpa took me camping down by the river. We hiked nearly all day to reach it."

"Ow!" Dokken yelled and slapped his hair. "Okay. What are these things?" he asked, examining the dead insect in his hand.

Litney looked briefly. "Deer flies."

Dokken began to swing his arms wildly around his face. "I hate them!" he shouted as he flailed his arms around at the swarm following him, and when he noticed Litney standing still, he demanded. "How can you stand it?"

Litney shrugged. Her mind was too busy to worry about the flies. Deer flies and horse flies were a fact of life in the country, especially on a farm.

The buzzing was about to drive him crazy. Dokken wanted to go home. What was he doing here anyway? How could something like this happen? How was he ever going to get home? Suddenly, his promise to stay with Litney seemed stupid. Angrily, Dokken persisted, "Do you remember the way? I can't keep going like this forever."

"Look, go back if you want. Go and sit with the perfect heron and ask your perfect questions and give your perfect answers."

Dokken grabbed her by the shoulder and stopped her. "Knock it off," he said. "I know you're scared, but that doesn't give you the right to be mean. I'm scared, too, okay? We have to make the best of this." When she didn't say anything, he got even more pointed. "So, Grufwin said some things you didn't understand, and he was questioning some things you believe. Yes, that's always uncomfortable. I get that, but I have a feeling the more open we keep our minds during this adventure, the better."

Litney turned, looked as if she were ready to fight, then flopped to the ground and began to cry.

Dokken didn't squat beside her, but he did sit near her. "What's wrong?"

"What if the bracelet . . ." she stopped for a moment. She could hardly bear to speak these words. "This bracelet is supposed to go to the daughters in my family, right? That much I know. But . . . what if, what if a daughter isn't . . . worthy?" She pulled up her knees, wrapped her arms around them and buried her face.

Dokken edged closer to her. He didn't know what to do or say. He felt like he never knew what to do or say, which is why he ate lunch all by himself every day. But he liked Litney, which meant he felt like he needed to do something. He reached his hand out slowly, as if he were about to touch a snake and kind of patted Litney's back, like his mom had when he'd hurt himself when he was a kid.

A noise behind them drew both of their attentions. It was a rustling in the grass. Both Litney and Dokken scrambled to their feet. "What is it?" he asked, his fearful voice betraying his city upbringing.

"I don't know," she said, wiping her eyes with the back of her hand and straining to see what was behind the tall grass. A dog leapt out, making them jump.

The dog was sleek, skinny really, and brown with big ears and eyes that were the oddest color Dokken and Litney had ever seen. Its eyes were a green that almost seemed to glow—like new leaves in spring. They weren't frightening, just intense. The dog didn't growl or bare its teeth. In fact, its long thin tail was wagging.

"Hey, pup," Litney said. "Hey there." She dropped into a squat and held out the back of her hand. The dog slowly came forward, gave her a sniff and then a lick. She scratched behind its ears, and the dog moaned in pleasure. Litney laughed.

"Looks like you've found a friend," Dokken said.

"She has," the dog answered.

"You know, we just got done talking with a blue heron, but I hadn't imagined that you'd be able to talk, too," Litney said. As she said that, something hovered at the back of her head, bothering her.

"You are the one," the dog said, pointing a nose toward her wrist.

"I have the bracelet," Litney said, still thinking it was some horrible mistake that she was the one on this adventure.

"I'm Mala," the dog said.

Litney couldn't help thinking that she had never seen a more beautiful dog. "I'm Litney. This is Dokken."

"He's your companion?" Mala asked, and the dog seemed surprised.

Litney nodded and said without looking at Dokken, "I've been really glad to have him along." Then she realized what had been bothering her. "You can talk."

"Clearly."

"But why couldn't Bernard, my grandparents' dog, talk? When he saw us, he barked and ran."

Mala nodded. "Animals that live with humans forget the ways of their world."

"Their world? What do you mean?" Litney asked.

"That'll take a bit of explaining, but you must be hungry," the dog said, looking at both of them.

"Starving," Dokken said.

Litney rubbed at her wrist and agreed since all she had had was some bread and jam early this morning and it was now, judging by the sun's position in the sky, past noon.

"Follow me, and I'll get you something to eat. Then we can talk about the ways of the world." The dog trotted off in a direction different from the one they had been heading. Dokken began to follow. Litney stopped him.

"What?" Dokken asked, one hand unconsciously on his stomach because now that he had been reminded of his hunger, he could think of nothing else.

"Mala's going away from the river. Grufwin said to go to the river and then head north."

"But maybe Mala's leading us someplace pretty close by. Plus, we won't be able to walk much further if we don't get something to eat."

Litney walked behind Dokken and noticed that Mala was leading them out of the fields and toward a small stand of trees.

"Dokken," she whispered.

"What?"

She could tell by his voice he was annoyed. "My bracelet is getting hot."

"It's probably just the sun." He walked faster. He needed food.

As they got closer to the trees, Litney couldn't keep her hand off her wrist. It was so hot, it was burning her. She was about to run to catch up with Dokken, since she had lagged quite a bit behind, when she saw a group of dogs burst out of the trees, barking, "Attack!" Mala was nowhere to be seen.

Dokken, terrified, stiffened, and he stood paralyzed in the middle of the field.

Litney knew what those dogs would do to him, so she picked up a large rock and ran in his direction. She knew it was rather pointless—a dog would have to be pretty close before she could throw her rock with any effect, and, even then, even if she sent one dog yelping for the trees, the others would reach her. Still, she didn't know what else to do.

She reached Dokken before the dogs could, and she stood in front of him, the rock in her left hand. "Don't run," she said over her shoulder. "Just stand there." She needn't have bothered. He was immobile.

As they got closer, the dogs slowed their headlong hurl and spread out into a crouching semi-circle. Litney's nervous legs wouldn't straighten the whole way, so she shifted back and forth, from one leg to the other. As scared as she was, she couldn't help noticing how striking these dogs were. They were some of the most beautiful animals she had ever seen, and traveling around the world with her mother to save endangered species, she had seen plenty. It was their eyes—they had the same glow that Mala's eyes had. She wondered what that meant.

"There isn't much meat between us," she told the dogs, gripping the rock.

One, a muscled black one on her left, answered, "You're right." The dogs continued their slow creep toward them.

"So what do you want with us?"

"That," the dog said, pointing his nose to her wrist.

"My bracelet? Why?"

"Because someone as stupid as you doesn't deserve to have something as powerful as that."

The dogs were at most fifteen feet away now. Litney could hear their harsh breathing. She knew there was no way to fight them all off with one rock. There were too many. She and Dokken would be torn to shreds. She heard Dokken whimper behind her—she guessed the only wild animals he had ever seen were behind bars at a zoo. It was up to her.

Or was it?

The bracelet on her wrist burned, and she looked down to see it had begun to glow. She followed its glow—it pointed to a tree just beyond the dogs and to her right. Keeping one eye on the dogs, she followed the beam that her bracelet was making, bright even in the noonday sun. It came to rest on something in the tree. Something brown and round—what was it? A nest? Yes, a wasps' nest. Litney's fear multiplied when she saw the beam was beginning to shake and bat at the nest. *Stop! We'll get stung!* she thought to herself, and then she understood. *Yes! We'll get stung. But so will the dogs.*

Wasps began to tumble from the vibrating nest and came hurtling down the beam of light. When Litney realized they were headed straight for her, she lowered her wrist until the shaft of light widened, spreading over all the dogs. The air began to roar with the sound of buzzing. The dog who had spoken to her realized what she had done and leapt at her. She swung hard and hit him with the rock, but not before his canine teeth found the flesh on the inside her wrist, just above the bracelet. Before the dog could do anything more, wasps, hundreds of angry wasps who could sting again and again and again, slammed into the dogs, going for their eyes, noses, anything fleshy and soft. Yelps and howls pierced through the buzzing, and Litney saw some wasps continuing along the ray of light all the way to her wrist. "Run!" she screamed at Dokken, dragging him by the arm when he didn't move.

The two of them ran, getting stung a few times by the wasps who followed them, but they escaped from the dogs that were now yelping and running back and forth across the field, much more concerned with the attack of the wasps than the two kids. While the stings hurt, Litney didn't care because, as they ran, the yelping grew more and more distant. The dogs, stung until their eyes swelled shut, were unable to follow. And the bracelet wasn't hot anymore.

They were still hungry and thirsty and her wrist was bleeding, but Litney and Dokken kept running.

34

* 6 *

The House

"I CAN'T," DOKKEN SAID, breathless. "I can't run anymore."

Litney didn't want to quit running because she knew the dogs still might be able to follow their scents, especially once the pain of the stings had subsided. But she also knew her own legs wouldn't be able to run much longer either. One last look behind them satisfied Litney that the dogs were not following them, at least for now. She slowed to a walk.

"You're bleeding."

Litney looked at her wrist. The blood had dried, turning from bright red to the color of bricks. "Yeah."

"Hey, Litney?" Dokken had stopped and was looking at her.

"Yeah?"

"I, uh, I didn't do anything."

She thought about playing dumb, but didn't. "Yes, you did."

"Don't lie. I just stood there like a big coward." He should have gone home. Things were not going to be any different here with her than they were back in his own life. Back there, people expected him to fail. He wasn't disappointing anyone because that's always what he did.

"But you helped me out at the pond with Grufwin. I didn't manage so well there, did I?" She could tell he wanted to argue with her—probably something about how she was a girl, so she added. "Plus, I had the bracelet."

"You picked up the rock before you figured out the bracelet was going to do anything."

"It's not a big deal. I'm used to animals on the farm. What we need to worry now about is food and water."

Dokken groaned. "I don't know which is worse—dying because of dogs attacking us or dying because of thirst."

"Thirst. It takes longer. Look—the good news is the fields are ending." It was true, the fields poured into a valley.

"Why is that good news?"

"You are a city boy. When the land dips down like that, it means we're near the river." They walked through tall grass and found a path that animals used to get down to the water. Sumac and other bushes grew on either side of them. "Oh, thank you! Thank you!" Litney exclaimed, jumping up and down.

"What?"

Litney pointed a finger toward the underbrush. Dokken could barely make out something dark hiding beneath the green leaves. "Blackberries," she informed him.

The bushes were thick with them, and soon the two of them were shoving plump explosions of juice into their mouths. They ate so quickly and ravenously that some of the black juice dribbled down their chins. Before long, the bushes were empty.

"Those were great . . ." Dokken said.

"But I'm still hungry," Litney finished, swiping at her chin with the back of her hand.

"Yep. So what do we do?"

"Keep walking."

Dokken sighed. "I was afraid you were gonna say that."

They started down the thin trail through the brush toward the river. "Hey, wait," Dokken said suddenly and Litney looked back.

"What?" she asked.

"Look. Over there."

Litney followed the line of Dokken's finger and could see something shiny off to their left and back up the hill. "What do you suppose that is?"

This time, it was Dokken who could tease, "Country girl. That's the sun reflecting off a window. New York City is nothing but."

"Maybe it's a house."

"I'm willing to walk back up this hill to find out," Dokken said.

When they got back to the top of the hill, they found a trail leading toward a tall house that had probably at one time been blue. A wide porch took up the entire front of the house, and a garage sat off by itself with an old car flanking it on each side.

"It doesn't look like anybody lives there," Litney said, not even trying to hide her disappointment.

"Yeah. Still, maybe we could find something."

"I guess."

The two of them walked toward the house, slowing more and more the closer they got.

Litney whispered, "This feels creepy."

Dokken nodded. "I say creepy all the time. It annoys my mom because she says what I call creepy is never really creepy. But this . . ." he paused. "This is really, really creepy."

"Let's walk around the house first."

"Good idea."

They did a slow circuit of the house. They found an elaborate gazebo out back with stubborn bits of white paint clinging to it, but no matter how they looked at it, the house was still old, run-down, and creepy. When they made it around to the front again, Dokken put his mouth close to Litney's ear. "Do you think we should go in?"

She shrugged. "I wouldn't except I'm so hungry."

"Do you really think there's going to be any food in there?"

"Probably not. But there might be some cans of food in the kitchen."

"Maybe," but Dokken did not look the least bit hopeful.

Litney approached the stairs leading up to the door. Dokken waited at the bottom of the steps while Litney slowly crossed the porch to the front door. She knocked. The wind shuffled through leaves on the one oak tree in the yard.

She knocked again, waited, then opened the screen door. After knocking once more on the inside door, she looked back at Dokken. He didn't say anything, so she turned the handle on the door. "It isn't locked."

Neither of them knew if that was good or bad.

Litney took a step inside. She had entered her own house before when it was empty, but this was different. This was more like stepping into a cemetery in the dark.

The screen door slapped behind Litney, and she jumped. When she looked back, she saw Dokken had crept up the steps and was sitting on the porch.

"Aren't you coming in?"

With a sheepish smile, he shook his head and stretched as if he were just beginning a vacation. "Nope. I think I'll enjoy the fresh country air while I have the chance."

Litney rolled her eyes at him, then turned to her left into a living room where a fine dust fogged the air, as if it were so thick on the furniture and floors that up seemed to be the only place it could find to settle. The wood floors were covered by faded rugs that ran almost all the way to the walls. A large pump organ, over by a dusty picture window, was so covered with dolls that the only way Litney could tell it was an organ were the black and white keys peeking between the skirts of the bodies positioned on top of it.

One wall of the living room was filled with masks—huge ones, black ones, metal ones, wooden ones. Some were plain. Others intricate. "You're a pretty one," she said, reaching out a finger to touch a wooden one that looked like a little boy.

"Thank you," the mask replied.

Litney gave a little yelp.

"You okay?" Dokken asked from the screen door.

"Yeah, but there's something with this house. Like it's magical. It's old, Dokken."

"No, really?"

"I mean, there isn't going to be any food."

He might have sworn.

"But I think I'll look around a little more, if that's okay."

"Okay. I guess I wouldn't mind sitting out here and resting for a while, so take your time." She heard a rhythmic creaking and guessed Dokken had sat down on the porch swing she had seen out of the corner of her eye.

On the living room wall opposite the masks, somebody had painted a tree. Looking more closely at it, Litney saw hidden amongst its leaves all kinds of animals: a puma, a toucan, a sloth. They seemed so real that Litney reached out a hand to touch the toucan. She could have sworn that instead of feeling a wall, she felt the giving softness of feathers.

39

"Hmmm," she said to no one in particular. She meandered back out into the hallway and crossed into the room on the other side. "A library." Every last bit of wall space in the room was covered with books— each entire wall, with several freestanding bookshelves that were almost as tall as Litney in the middle of the room. There was even a desk with every square inch completely stacked fifteen and twenty books high. Litney looked at the books in the first bookcase and didn't recognize any of the titles: *The Golden Age of Crickets, Sky Down Ground Up,* and *What Is Ahead?* This last one sounded helpful, so she opened it up and read,

> *When need is to know*
> *out you go*
>
> *into the hands of rain where*
> *you will find*
>
> *a way to make all that is wrong*
> *fade*

It didn't make any sense to her, but she liked how it sounded, so she read it aloud. "When need is to know, out you go into the hands of rain . . ." She felt like saying it again, and this time, as she got to the end, "The way to make all that is wrong fade," she found she didn't even need to look at the book.

She put the book back, wishing she had days to go through this house—to see what secrets it might reveal—but she was so hungry that she wanted to get back to Dokken and continue looking for food. "But I might as well take a look in the kitchen. Just in case."

She walked down the hall, and this time, she didn't just gasp, she screamed. Dokken whipped open the screen door and came running down the hall. "What? What is it? What?"

Her hand on her heart, Litney pointed to a figure wearing an old-fashioned dress standing in the hall. "It's only a mannequin," she managed. "I thought it was real. I could have sworn I saw it moving."

"Let's get out of here," Dokken said, looking over his shoulder as if to make sure he could still see the way out. "This place scares me."

"Yeah, but let me look in the kitchen," Litney said. "Just in case."

"I can't stand it in here," Dokken told her. "I'm going back outside. Call me if you need me."

Litney moved toward the kitchen and tentatively pushed the swinging door open. No surprises it seemed, so she stepped inside. Even though she knew it was going to be the case, she was disappointed to see the empty cupboards in front of her (they had no doors, so their emptiness was obvious). In the middle of the room was a small table and two chairs. To her left was a huge black stove that Litney guessed must have been a wood stove, since a chimney led up to the ceiling. To the right was a wall full of pictures, a butter churner, and a huge old tortoise shell.

"Oh, well," she muttered, about to go through the swinging door once again.

"Greetings," a voice said.

One would have guessed she would have been used to surprises in this house, but still, Litney jumped and then twisted around and around, searching for something, anything that could have spoken. She thought of the mannequin she had passed in the hall, but she was certain the voice had come from this room.

"Greetings," the voice repeated, and this time, Litney knew that it had come from her right. She searched the pictures and while every one of them seemed to be staring at her, none looked as if it had spoken.

"Greetings!" and Litney knew she was meant to answer, even if she couldn't see who or what was speaking.

"Hello?"

"Better. Much better. When I was young, we knew we were supposed to answer our elders."

Litney wanted to ask how she was supposed to know she was speaking to an elder when she couldn't see to whom she was speaking, but the thought of Grufwin's disappointed face stopped her. "I'm sorry. I was trying to find who I was talking to."

"Yes, you humans always need to know that, don't you?"

It sounded like a rhetorical question, so Litney didn't answer but continued to search for where the voice might be coming from.

"Don't you?"

"Y-yes. I guess." Litney didn't know if she had ever been more perplexed by a situation. "Where are you? Who are you?" She suddenly realized it could be anything talking to her—a picture, spider, mouse with teeth stronger than walls.

"You are about to step on me."

Litney looked down and saw a head peeking out of the shell she had thought empty. "Oh—hello. Sorry about that."

"I'm Trembla," the tortoise said.

"That's a beautiful name."

The tortoise nodded and then pointed her pointy nose toward Litney's wrist. "The one must also have a name."

"I'm Litney."

"Did I hear you talking with someone out in the hall after you screamed?"

Litney blushed. "I swore the mannequin moved. I screamed, and my friend Dokken came in to see if I was okay."

Trembla peered behind Litney. Litney looked as well, and saw that Dokken wasn't there.

"Oh, he went back outside to sit down and rest."

"You were right. About the mannequin. That's Empira. She keeps house. You probably scared her stiff." Trembla chuckled at her own joke.

Litney remembered the dust. "She cleans?"

"No, she doesn't clean. She keeps the house. She makes sure the dolls have tea for their parties and that the animals in the jungle are warm enough. Things like that." The tortoise looked closely at Litney. "What are you thinking, child?'

"That sounds rather boring," Litney confessed.

"Nothing is boring if you love doing it."

"But how can you love something if it's boring? I'm sorry," Litney immediately apologized. "I shouldn't argue."

"Whyever not?"

She thought again of Grufwin. "It can seem impolite."

"If you always have to be right, yes. But if you are truly trying to understand something, no."

Litney collapsed on the floor. "I don't get it."

The tortoise's eyes had great kindness in them. "Not many do. So, you are hungry."

"Yes." Litney didn't know the hunger pains were beginning to make her shoulders round.

"How would you like something to eat?"

"But—" Litney said.

"Another hint is to always answer the question at hand."

"I would love to eat."

Trembla said, "Humans have a saying, 'You can't get something for nothing.' Is that it?"

Litney's answer was a wary, "Yes."

"If you can do three things, you will eat."

"What about Dokken?"

"Your concern is admirable. He'll eat as well. Now, at the table you'll find a piece of paper and a variety of drawing utensils. I want you to draw fear."

"You mean something that makes me afraid?" Litney clarified as she stood up.

"Is that what I asked?"

Litney felt like she was having a conversation with her mother. "You have to *lis*-ten," her mother was always saying. "No, that isn't what you said. You said 'Draw fear.' But—"

Trembla pointed her nose toward the table.

Litney was careful not to let the huff out as she sat down. How in the world was she supposed to draw fear? How stupid. She kicked one foot against the leg of the table and tucked one leg under the other. She put her head down on the table. Not knowing what else to do, she let her mind wander. It made its way back to the confrontation with the dogs. As they had approached with their snarling faces, the fear had gone the entire length of her body—from the hairs on her head raising slightly to her toes clenching. Lifting her head, she ran her hand over the crayons, markers, pencil, pen, and stopped on a piece of artist's charcoal. She had never used charcoal before, but her mother had a charcoal drawing of a tree in her office. It was haunting.

Picking up the charcoal, she made broad strokes the length of the paper—they were sharp and clean until here and there, she smudged the lines a little, as if there were little clouds coming off them. In the center of the commotion of lines, she drew a black circle and filled it in. She made the circle a little bigger, and then took her index finger and began rubbing in a circular motion—bigger, bigger, bigger until the black nearly covered the page. There were still moments of pure white on her page—just as she could remember the beautiful sunshine filtering through the trees even as the dogs had advanced—but the black was powerful and pervasive.

"Here," she said, showing the paper to Trembla.

"What color is justice?" the tortoise asked, without commenting on the picture Litney had drawn.

It was getting harder and harder to concentrate, what with the hunger and everything that had happened so far. "Hmm?"

"What color is justice?"

Litney doubted she was going to get any food—where was it after all, and how was a tortoise going to cook, and who knew if her picture looked like fear? Still, she forced her mind to focus. "What color is justice?" She tried to list off different colors in her head, but all she could think was red and blue. Red and blue. Finding another sheet of paper, she took a pen and wrote, "Red, blue, yellow, green, black, white, gray, purple, orange, brown." Then she said, "Red. Red is rage and blue is . . . I don't know. Yellow? Green is money. Black is night. White is nothing. Gray is the middle. Purple is what kings and queens wear. Orange? Brown? Isn't brown what I get when I mix all of my paints together?" She couldn't remember so she tried another direction. "Justice. What is justice? Justice is what's fair. What's fair for everyone. You take away sides and come together. All you worry about is what's right. What's equal. Maybe it's brown—since that's what happens when all the colors are mixed together. No one stands out or gets extra treatment. Like water and dirt. It's no longer 'I am water' and 'I am dirt'—they work together to make something new."

Trembla asked, "What is your answer, child?"

"Brown." Whenever she took tests, Litney knew when she had an answer right and when she had an answer wrong. She knew she was wrong. How in the world could justice be brown? Yes, it was the color of her eyes, but everyone knew it was the most boring color in the world.

Knowing it was already over, Litney asked, "Since I've gotten the first two questions wrong, do I even need to try and answer the third one?"

"That is up to you."

"Fine," she sighed. "Ask."

"Do you want something hot or cold?"

"What? I don't understand. I can't think anymore." Litney lowered her head and began to cry.

"My dear, do you want something to eat that is hot or cold?" Trembla asked, gently.

"I-I-I don't care," Litney said.

"Litney, look up."

When she did, the table was covered with platters and dishes and plates of food. Even though absolute hunger had rushed into her mouth, she did have the presence of mind to ask, "Is this enchanted food? I mean, am I going to take one bite and long for it the rest of my life? Or will it put me into a deep and dreamless sleep until some prince comes to kiss me and wake me up?" She thought of Dokken having to kiss her and made a face.

Trembla laughed. "Child, you have been reading too many stories. It's good food. I promise."

To her credit, before she ate even one bite, Litney rose from the table. "I need to get Dokken. He's hungrier than I am."

"By all means, Litney."

As HE SAT OUTSIDE, DOKKEN WAS sure Litney would return with the bad news that there was nothing to eat. He rubbed his stomach as he stared out into the fields surrounding him and what he was seeing reminded him of books he had read about the Native Americans. Those books were his favorite kind, and in fact, he had an entire shelf of them in his room back in New York City. He had read all about the different tribes—the ones who lived in the mountains, the ones who rode across the rolling plains and hunted buffalo. Rolling plains just like this one. He could almost see the buffalo roaming and grazing in these soft hills. He imagined himself sitting astride a bareback pony and galloping around with a bow on his back and the wind in his face. What that must have felt like. That big freedom under that big sky. No fences, no roads. Just cloud and hoof and grass.

With a surprising and sudden surge, Dokken felt strong and powerful. Like he could do anything he set his mind to. He stood up to go explore a little more, to go out and get them some food, but then the door opened. He turned and Litney was there, saying with a smile, "Time to eat."

* 7 *

Magic

FOOD OF ALL SHAPES, COLORS, and consistencies quenched any last fingerings of hunger Dokken and Litney might have felt. They had been too hungry to ask what they were eating, and it had tasted too good to care.

When their stomachs pushed pleasantly against their belly skin, they sat back. "Trembla," Litney said. "Thanks. That was great."

"Yeah," Dokken agreed in a dazed sort of way. "Yeah."

They all laughed.

"I guess we were pretty hungry," Litney said.

"Yes, you were," Trembla said.

"I was so worried because I didn't think I had gotten the answers right."

"You didn't."

"But—I don't—why did we get the food?" an anxious Litney asked.

"I didn't say you got the answers wrong either."

Dokken said, "Talking with you animals makes my head hurt. It feels like everything is a riddle."

"It could be because animals are less concerned with right and wrong."

"So, why have a test? A test implies right and wrong," Litney said.

Trembla answered, "Not necessarily. A test can mean an ordeal. It can also mean a reaction. Or proof. Litney, you gave your answers, and you had very good reasons for choosing the answers you did. Someone else might have had a different drawing or a different answer and it would have been just as valuable. For example, Dokken, what color is justice?"

"That's what you had to answer to get us this food?" Dokken asked.

"Yep."

"Gosh, what color is justice? I'd say blue."

"Why?" Litney asked.

"Because it is like the sky—it covers everything. Whether we're good or bad, a tree or a person, we're all under it. What color did you say, Litney?"

"Brown."

"Really? Brown?" Dokken asked. "I'd never have considered that."

"If you mix all the colors together, if you mix water and dirt together, it makes everything brown. It evens everything out. No one gets special treatment."

"Oh. Sure, I can see that," Dokken said.

Trembla nodded, and then after a moment, she said, "Oh. I did forget to mention one thing?"

"What's that?" Litney asked.

"This food *was* magical."

"You told me it wasn't!" Litney cried, beginning to be alarmed.

"No, I told you it was good food. And it was, wasn't it?"

"Yes. Delicious," Dokken answered.

"So, how is it magical?" Litney wanted to know.

"You'll not need to eat for the rest of your adventure," Trembla answered.

"Really? We won't get hungry?" Dokken asked.

"No, you will not get hungry."

"Cool," Dokken said, looking at Litney, who nodded.

"But . . ." Trembla said.

"Why is there always a but?" Litney asked, but she was smiling.

"But, if you do eat any other food on your adventure—anything from a blackberry to the smallest crumb of bread—you will know a hunger a hundred times worse than what you felt when you arrived here."

"Why?" Dokken asked.

"Was the food good?"

"Yes," they both answered, and Dokken added, "Better than anything I've ever eaten before."

"Then it is enough for you to know that you have been filled, and so you need not search for anything else to fill you. Now," Trembla said, "it's getting dark, and so I'd suggest you spend the night here."

Litney said nothing, but her eyes questioned Dokken. He was thinking the house was still a little creepy, but not nearly as bad as it had been when they had first been walking around. "I'm okay with that," he said.

Trembla told them, "Empira will show you to the Sunset Room. Sleep well, children. You'll need it."

Litney bent down on one knee and bowed her head. "Thank you."

Trembla touched the top of the girl's head with her own. "You are welcome, Litney. May every blessing bless you and no strength fail you. Go on, now."

Litney rose and followed Dokken out into the hall.

"Oh, my, hello!" Empira the mannequin said to them without her lips moving.

"Hello," the children said.

"Let me show you to your room." They followed her to a place behind the stairs where she pushed back a sliding door, revealing an elevator. "It's hard for me to make it up the stairs," she explained.

All three stepped in, and the elevator rose quickly enough to make their stomachs lurch.

"Whee," Empira said with her mouth frozen in a smile. It would have been a little freaky if she hadn't had such nice eyes.

"We'll put you in the Sunset Room," Empira said as they stepped out of the elevator. They followed her down to the door at the end of the hallway. "Here it is."

The sun, which was setting as they entered, spent its rich gold recklessly in this room. Windows made up the entire west wall, and sunlight poured in, washing the room in golden light.

"It's beautiful," Litney whispered.

Empira nodded stiffly, but her voice was soft. "Isn't it? And look behind you."

For a moment, both Dokken and Litney thought the east wall was covered with mirrors, because it reflected perfectly the shifting colors of the sky.

"It's not a mirror," Dokken exclaimed after he had touched it. "It's a wall. Just like any other."

"Well, not quite like any other," Empira said with that smile.

"How's it doing that?" Litney asked. "Hey, and speaking of, how do you talk? You aren't an animal."

"Animals aren't the only beings who can talk in this world. Now, I assume the two of you want separate beds?" Empira pointed to the large queen bed covered with pillows.

"Well, uh," Dokken blushed. He didn't want to, but still he offered, "I could sleep in a different room."

"No need," and suddenly the bed split into two halves. Pointing to a door, she said, "There's a bathroom right there. You'll find towels, bubbles, toothbrushes, and anything else you want."

"What about hot chocolate?" Litney teased.

"Go see."

Litney opened the door and sitting on a silver tray on the sink were two mugs of hot chocolate overflowing with marshmallows.

"Wow, cool."

"No, it should be hot," Empira said, dipping a stiff pinky finger into the froth.

Dokken and Litney laughed. "We say cool when something is neat or good."

"Oh," Empira said. "Cool."

Litney hugged her, surprising them both. "Thanks, Empira."

"You are welcome, Litney. You are needed, and so anything I can do to help you will help all."

Litney's face lost its smile. "Yeah."

"I take it by your face that you're afraid?" Empira asked.

"Yes. I mean, whatever I'm supposed to do sounds so big, so important. What if I mess up?"

"We all 'mess up,'" Empira said, trying out another foreign phrase.

"But it feels like I'm supposed to be saving the world. It isn't good to mess up when you're doing that," Litney said. She twisted a piece of hair at the back of her neck.

"I think that if we're any good at all, we're all trying to save the world—in our own ways."

"Kind of like a basketball game," Dokken said. "It isn't just the last-second shot that decides the game—it's every play and every player up to that point."

"I guess I hadn't thought of it that way," Litney said.

"Neither had I," Empira said. "Well put, Dokken. Please let me know if you need anything. Good night." Empira left the room, closing the door behind her.

"I've never shared a room with a girl before," Dokken said, trying to make a joke, but his discomfort was plain.

"I've never been fed by a tortoise and shown to my bedroom by a talking mannequin either." Litney giggled. "It's . . . it's weird, isn't it?"

"It sure is. I'm still scared most of the time, but it's kind of been fun."

"I know. I worry it won't stay like that for long, though."

"Probably not," Dokken agreed.

53

"Well," Litney said, looking around, "Would you like to take a shower first or do you want me to?"

"Take a shower? Why in the world would I want to do that?"

Litney scanned his body from head to toe. She started to laugh. "Because you're filthy."

"So?"

"It might be a week or even a month until you can take a shower again."

"I repeat, so?"

Litney chose to be blunt. "You're going to stink soon. Plus, you'll get your nice bed all dirty."

She could tell he wanted to argue with her, and so she was surprised when he said, "Fine. I'll take a shower."

WHILE DOKKEN TOOK A SHOWER, Litney sat in a chair looking out the bank of windows. She reached for her hot chocolate. As the cup touched her lips, she jerked it away, recalling Trembla's warning about not eating any food. She hadn't said anything about drinks—did they count? "Better not try," Litney said, putting the cup down. The hot chocolate smelled so good, this was nearly impossible to do.

Litney got up, hesitated, then knocked on the bathroom door. "Hey, Dokken—."

"I just got in here."

"I know. I wanted to ask if you had any hot chocolate?"

"No. I was saving it for after," he yelled back. "Why?"

"Don't drink any, okay?"

"Why not?"

"Remember what Trembla said?" Litney asked.

There was a pause. "But she said *food.*"

"I know, but I'm not sure what hot chocolate is. I just want to be safe instead of sorry."

"Aw, man," Dokken said. "I guess you're right. It sure does smell good though."

"I know."

"I'll be done in a minute," he told her. "Or at least I think I will. This feels awfully good."

"Don't worry. I'm not in a hurry."

Litney returned to her chair. The sun was gone, but she noticed the room was still light which was odd, because there weren't any lights on. Looking behind her, Litney saw that the wall continued to glow with the colors of the sun. "Awesome," she thought. And then, "What a day!" as her mind slipped from to the smell of roses, to the crows, to the dogs and the blackberries. She thought of Trembla, Mala. Without thinking, she rubbed the bracelet and wondered what her mother and grandmother were doing. She wondered if they had been in this house, eaten Trembla's food.

Dokken opened the door, wearing his clothes. "I was going to tell you it was stupid to take a shower and then put on my dirty clothes again."

"But your clothes are clean," Litney said with wonder.

He looked down at himself, pulling his shirt out to see for sure. It was perfectly clean. "Must have happened while I was in the shower."

"This is the weirdest house in the world."

Dokken said only half-jokingly, "If it *is* in the world."

"Hey, Dokken, I was thinking. It seems like we can get things in this room or house."

"Like the food and the hot chocolate."

"And your clothes. I mean, it sort of seems like this house might be preparing us for the rest of the adventure."

"Yeah, our fairy god-house."

Litney grinned. "And so I was wondering if there was anything we thought we might need for the rest of the journey."

"A gun," Dokken said, thinking about the dogs.

"I had thought of that, but I don't want a gun. I'm not sure I have the guts to use it, and, plus, so much can go wrong with one."

"What about a knife?" Dokken asked.

Litney nodded. "One of those might be good to have."

"What else?"

"Trembla said we didn't need to worry about food anymore, but what about a canteen for water?" Litney suggested.

"And how about a first aid kit?" Dokken asked, pointing to Litney's arm.

"And rope."

"This is probably the last night we'll be able to spend inside," Dokken said, thinking.

"So . . . a tent and two blankets."

"Yeah."

"Anything else?" Litney asked.

"A flashlight."

"Oh, I'm glad you thought of that," Litney said looking out the windows at the very dark night. "Yes, a flashlight could be handy."

"It's not like I need one," Dokken said, quietly, "but a walking stick would be cool."

Litney nodded. "All right. So a knife, a canteen, some rope, a tent, two blankets, a flashlight, a walking stick . . . is that it?"

"And a first aid kit," Dokken said, holding up a finger.

"Right. So . . ." Litney paused.

"What?" Dokken asked.

"I don't know what to do."

Dokken shrugged. "Maybe say we'd love to have those things—please."

Feeling silly, Litney cleared her throat and spoke loudly, her nose pointed up toward the ceiling. "For our adventure, we would like to have a knife, a canteen, some rope, a tent, two blankets, a flashlight, a walking stick, and a first aid kit. Please. Thanks."

"How are we going to know if it worked?"

"If we find the stuff or not."

They waited for a minute or two. Nothing happened, so Litney said, "I'm going to take my shower. Let me know if anything 'appears.'"

"Okay."

Litney went into the bathroom and closed the door. The steam from Dokken's shower was just beginning to dissipate, and in the mirror, she could make out the bottom half of her face. It was streaked with dirt and a little blood. As she undressed, she felt good. While she was scared about what the next day would bring, she felt like . . . like she had finally done something. As the water poured over her, she even brought up her arm and flexed her bicep. Her muscle made a little bulge, and she growled as if she were a tough tiger. Then she laughed. At herself. At the situation. At the sheer weirdness of life.

The shower ranked right up there with the food as one of those things she would be forever grateful for and never forget. The heat dissolved all the stings and aches, and she had no idea how long she stood under the spray. It seemed like hours. It felt wonderful.

Her clothes were clean when she stepped out of the shower, and lying beside them were two leather knapsacks. Dressing quickly, she opened the door. "Look what I found."

"How do we know whose is whose?"

Litney looked at them. "This one has a picture of the bracelet on it. That's probably mine."

"What's on this one?" Dokken asked.

"It looks like a snake? Or maybe a stick."

Dokken didn't hide his disappointment well. "But there's no walking stick. One obviously couldn't fit inside."

Litney unclasped her knapsack. "I have a blanket, a knife, a flashlight, a tent."

Dokken pulled out the contents of his. "I have a first aid kit, rope, a blanket, and . . . and—"

"And what?"

"A walking stick," he exclaimed, pulling out a stick nearly as tall as he was. "I'm not sure why this amazes me."

It felt like Christmas morning. "Thank you," Litney said loudly.

"Yes. Thanks."

"Well . . . I suppose we should get some sleep."

"I'm exhaus—" Dokken's yawn stopped him from finishing the word.

They climbed into their beds, and the sunset wall dimmed a little. "Good night," Litney said.

"Good night," Dokken answered around another yawn.

"I know I said it earlier, but I am really glad you're here," Litney whispered. "I'd be scared to death without you."

Dokken had already started to snore softly.

8

The Rock

*L*ITNEY KNEW SHE WAS COMING out of a deep and wonderful sleep, but couldn't imagine why. She tried snuggling back under the blankets, hoping she might return to the dreams that had left a small smile on her face all night. But something was waking her. For starters, the bed was growing uncomfortable. Maybe she was being the ungrateful princess with the pea, but something was poking her right shoulder blade.

And what was that? It sounded like a bird was in the room. She hadn't noticed any cage the night before.

Her eyes opened to a dull greenish tan of a ceiling that was so close she could reach out and touch it. "Huh?" she asked.

Dokken groaned beside her and mumbled, "Just a minute more, Mom."

Litney elbowed him. "Dokken, get up."

He sat up with a jerk. For a long moment, he stared around him. "Hmm? What? Hey, we're in a tent."

"Yes."

"But we were in a house," Dokken said.

"I know." Litney unzipped the flaps and stepped outside. "There's no house," she said when she ducked back inside.

"No house at all?"

"Nope. We're on the hill where the house was. I can tell by that big oak over there, but there isn't a building in sight."

"So was it real?"

Litney gestured to the walls around her, "If it wasn't, how did we get this?"

Dokken didn't answer, just rubbed his eyes.

As Litney watched him, she decided there was no word more appropriate to describe his hair than a shock of orange. She pulled her brown hair back into a ponytail and said, "There isn't much else to do, so how 'bout we pack up and head out?"

They decided to walk down the hill toward the river. The sun was half above, half below the horizon, and as it quickly pulled itself up into the sky, the red leaking all over the sky began to pale.

"It feels really odd not to eat," Litney commented. "This is the third time I have caught myself chewing on my tongue just because my mouth wants something to do."

"I was just thinking that. I'm not hungry or anything, but my mom always made me eat breakfast. No matter how late we were."

"Were you late often?"

"All the time," Dokken admitted. "I was late so often in fact, that my teachers gave up on punishing me for it."

"It's just the opposite in my family. I once had a doctor's appointment, and we got there forty-five minutes early."

"Forty-five minutes early. Why?"

Litney shrugged. "I have no idea."

They passed by the blackberry bushes they had eaten from the night before. "They're full of berries again," Dokken noticed. "They couldn't have grown berries back that quickly, could they?"

"Not without magic."

Close to the river, the path made a steep descent and they were soon right next to the water. "Does the path keep going?" Dokken asked from behind.

"It looks like it does, at least for a while. Grufwin said to stay on this side, right?"

"Until we get to the Rock that Boils."

Litney said, "I sure hope we know the rock when we see it. Did Grufwin say how far we needed to go to get to the rock?"

"No. Only that we were supposed to stay on this side of the river until we got there."

They walked on, commenting on the weeping willows that hung down into the water, pointing out the hawks circling in the sky above them, but neither of them noticed something large and dark that seemed to be following them in the water.

"I'M THIRSTY. HOW 'BOUT A DRINK?" Dokken asked, leaning against a tree. The two of them had been fighting the overgrown weeds along the path for over an hour.

"Sounds good." Litney sat down on a rock. It jutted out from the shore, creating a little peninsula that curved out into the river like a U. The river's water, hitting the obstacle, began to turn on itself and bubble. Litney rubbed her wrist and took the canteen Dokken offered. "Mmm, that's good."

Dokken took a long drink and then asked, "Do you think we should fill it up here?"

Litney looked at the river. It was clear but brown. "I don't know. What do you think?"

Dokken looked in the canteen. "We don't have to."

"Okay. Let's wait and see if we find something cleaner."

"No, I mean we don't have to. The canteen's full again."

Litney reached for the canteen and closed one eye to peek in its little hole. "Magic."

"Really-useful-to-have magic," Dokken clarified. "Hey, is your wrist bothering you? You're rubbing it a lot."

"Yeah, the bracelet is getting hot again."

"Uh oh."

"What?"

"You told me it was getting hot right before the dogs came out of the trees. Remember?"

Litney didn't answer, but stood and scanned the river, the trees. "I don't see anything." Her wrist was turning red. "I can hardly stand it."

"Maybe put your hand in the water. That might help until we figure out what's going on."

She knew she couldn't take the bracelet off to try to get some relief, so Dokken's idea sounded as good as any. Litney sat down and plunged her hand into the bubbling water. As soon as she did, the water calmed until it was smooth. Like a mirror. She noticed something shimmery growing in the mirror, as if it were walking closer to her.

When the light had grown bright enough to make her squint, a voice asked, "Why are you here?"

"Ummm . . . because we were tired and needed to rest."

"Why do you think small?" the light asked.

How was she supposed to answer that?

When she didn't say anything, the light repeated the first question. "Why are you here?"

She tried to imagine how Grufwin or Trembla might answer. "The bracelet found me."

The light flickered. "Why do you say the bracelet found you?"

Litney thought back to the garage sale. "Because I never go to garage sales. Because everyone says it is too early. It wasn't anything I did."

"How do you feel about the bracelet?"

"At first I didn't want it," Litney admitted.

"Why?"

She thought about lying. "Because it seemed important to my mother."

"Why should that matter?"

"Because *I* want to be important to my mother."

"Are you?"

Litney looked away. "It doesn't feel like it sometimes."

"Are you important to your mother?"

Litney squirmed. "Yes."

"Does your mother do good?"

"I suppose."

The light grew brighter and the voice grew stronger. "Does your mother do good?"

Litney thought about how hard her mother worked to save animals and insects from extinction, creatures that would have otherwise ceased to exist. "Yes."

"Why are you here?" the light asked for a third time.

She wanted to say she had already answered that. She wanted to ask the light why it only asked questions. The bracelet tingled on her arm, making her skin feel nervous. Or like it was stuck in a pool full of bubbles. Bubbles—she had seen them while sitting on the rock . . . and they had looked exactly like the ones in a pot when she was helping her parents cook. That was it. She was at the Rock that Boils. "I'm here to learn why I'm here."

"What do you need to learn?"

"I thought you'd tell me," Litney answered honestly.

"What do you need to learn?"

For a moment she wished she was back in the normal world, where everyone talked normally, where there were normal answers to normal questions. Answers that she knew. She had never before wished to be taking a math test, but even that would be easier than this because then she knew there would be an answer. "I don't know." She let her head hang, sure the Rock would send her back home, a failure.

"Why do you think it's bad to say you don't know?"

"Because you're asking me a question, and you want an answer."

"Must every question be answered?"

"I know not all questions *can* be answered, but that doesn't stop us from wanting an answer or trying to find an answer."

The light shimmered again, and Litney wished she knew what that meant. "What is a question you can't answer?"

"Why you shimmer sometimes when I answer."

"Why do you think I shimmer?"

"Because of my answers. Because they're wrong."

"What if it is because I sneezed?" This time the light waved and danced wildly for a moment before settling back into its normal brightness.

"Were you laughing?" Litney asked.

"Yes."

"Hey, that's the first time you haven't asked me a question."

"And that's the first time you haven't worried about what you were saying." The light moved a little closer. "Litney, how do you feel about the bracelet now?"

"I'm amazed by it. I don't understand it. I want to be worthy of it." The last she said in a whisper.

"Do you have any idea why you're here?"

"Not really," Litney said. "Everyone seems to think it's very important though because I'm only fourteen instead of sixteen."

"I'll tell you why you're here, but I can only tell you what I'm going to tell you. Nothing more. Nothing less."

"All right."

"As you've noticed, you're in a different world. It might look like the same world—river, fields—but it's different. That's why animals can speak, why houses can appear and disappear. While this may be difficult for you to grasp and even harder to accept, it doesn't end there. There are, in fact, many different worlds, all right next to one another. In most cases, no one from one world can enter another world. That is unless they find a key. I don't mean an actual key like the one that lets you into a house. It could be a book, a rock, a mushroom, some sort of thing that lets a being in one world move into another. Does that make sense?'

Litney nodded.

The light continued. "And there are two different kinds of keys. There is a key that lets you go from one world only into the very next one. Kind of like a key to a specific office door. The only door it opens is the one for that office. But there's another key—a master key if you will. That kind of key can let you into any world you want. This master key is extremely rare. I know of only two. The bracelet is that kind of key. We don't know where the bracelet came from, how it got its power or why it has chosen to appear to the women in your family. Nor are we sure exactly why you are here now, two years early. Our best guess is that a creature from another world has found its way to this world and has somehow conjured up the bracelet, gotten it to come early."

"Why?"

"Because if the creature got the bracelet, it would have access to all the different worlds. And," the light dimmed slightly, "some creatures, who are nothing special in their own worlds, can suddenly gain great power in other worlds. That's why the bracelet is so valuable. This has never happened before. The other women in your family . . . their experiences with the bracelet were far different from what yours will be. When your ancestors have visited our world in the past, it was more of a . . . a tour instead of a quest. Each was shown the sights they needed to see to show them the importance of their mission back in your world. For instance, your grandmother was shown a world where food was a pill that people swallowed so they didn't know what it was they were eating and they didn't get to enjoy the taste and flavors in their mouths. Your mother was given a bottle to feed the last briti here on earth. The soft little thing died in her lap. While neither of these experiences were pleasant, neither were they dangerous.

"Litney, before I go any further, do you know you can say no to this?"

Litney nodded.

"But do you really believe it?"

Litney said, "I feel as if everyone would be very disappointed in me, but I really believe if I so chose, I could say no."

"Then this is what you must know. This creature that we think is after the bracelet is called Mala."

"I met Mala," Litney said. "She was the most beautiful dog I have ever seen."

"And what happened?"

Litney answered, "She led us to the trees, where we were attacked by some other dogs."

The light grew intense. "Did they say anything to you?"

"They wanted the bracelet." Litney's face burned, "They said someone as stupid as me didn't deserve something as powerful as the bracelet."

"They do know how to hurt, don't they? Litney, in the past, we have had everything planned for the Way girls. We have known exactly where to send them and what to do. That is not so with you. We don't know how to tell you to proceed. Mala knows who you are and what you have. Like I said, we think she brought you and the bracelet here early. What we can guess is that she'll do anything to get her hands on the bracelet. Do you understand what I mean?"

Litney nodded slowly and then her eyes shifted to the bracelet. "Can't I just take the bracelet off and go back home? She can't get into our world without it, right?"

"Yes, she could . . . if she found another key. And the keys that let you go from one world directly into the next are not all that rare. She could find one quickly and easily."

"But still, wouldn't it be better for me to face her in my world instead of this one?" Litney was thinking she could have her mother and grandmother's help that way.

"No. For whatever reason, the bracelet has decided to appear now, and it has brought you here. That means that whatever is to happen is supposed to take place now and in this world."

"But what am I supposed to do?"

The light shimmered again. "I'm afraid you have to go out and find Mala."

"Then what?" Litney asked, trying not to tremble.

"You must face her and hopefully defeat her. If she gets that bracelet . . ." the light flashed then grew very dark. "Well, we can't think about that. Whatever else happens, do not let Mala get the bracelet. That's all I can tell you about your task." The light paused. "Will you accept it?"

How could Litney survive an encounter with a creature like Mala who was determined to do anything to get the bracelet and was as dangerous as any other wild predator? Still, the bracelet had protected her from the dogs in the field. And if Litney didn't use the bracelet, who could? It only came to her family, and so far, it had kept her safe. If it was willing to use her, then she was willing to trust it. "I need to know about Dokken."

"He has already been given his own chance to make a choice. When you return to him, however, you can tell him in more detail what you face, and he can have one last choice to leave."

"Will either of us—"

"I can answer no more, but now I must have your answer."

She whispered, "I'll do it."

* 9 *

A Fish, a Skunk, and a Bear

*L*ITNEY! LITNEY!"

She opened her eyes and saw orange that slowly transformed into Dokken's face and hair. Her head hurt, and she realized she was on her back. "What happened?" she asked as she sat up.

Dokken sat back on his haunches and ran a shaking hand through his hair. "I don't know. I told you to put your hand in the water. You did, and then you froze up. I thought you were having a seizure or something like this kid Jackson does at my school, but you weren't moving. At all. I checked your breath, your pulse. Nothing. But you didn't fall over or anything until right before you snapped out of it. I . . . . I thought you had died."

Litney pointed to the water swirling beside her. "The Rock That Boils."

This time it was Dokken's turn to ask, "What happened?"

"When I put my hand in the water, it went still. Completely still. Like a mirror. And then this light approached me."

69

"Someone was carrying a light?"

"No, it was just . . . light. It started out asking me all of these questions, and then it asked me if I was ready for what was ahead of me." She told him what the light had said, about Mala and the different kinds of keys, about how her journey was going to be more dangerous than her mother's or grandmother's.

"You are supposed to go out and *find* Mala, even though she probably wants to kill you for the bracelet?" he asked, pointing to her arm.

"Yep."

"Why?" Dokken asked.

"Because if Mala gets her hands on this bracelet, it means she can go into any world she wants."

"That's not that big a deal, is it?" Dokken said.

"The light said some creatures who have no power in their own world can be very powerful in other worlds," Litney answered.

"So, if Mala got the bracelet, she could go into any world and what, destroy it?"

"Possibly. I don't know. What matters is that we make sure Mala doesn't get the bracelet," Litney said.

"And how do we do that?"

"We have to destroy her."

Dokken laughed, but then he realized Litney was serious, and he turned a little ashen. "Look," he said, "this isn't some movie. Those dogs were obviously working for Mala, and they were not inviting us to dinner. They were going to kill us to get the bracelet. Do you hear me? *Kill* us."

"I know," Litney said.

"Like dead. Like our bodies bloody and torn and shredded and—"

"I know!" Litney shouted.

Dokken insisted, "This is dangerous."

"I know!" Litney repeated, more softly this time. "But, look, the bracelet comes to my family, and it came to me. That means it's up to me to protect it, and if I have to protect it by destroying Mala, then that's what I have to do."

"What if you fail?" Dokken asked.

Litney would not cry. "I can't fail."

"But—" Dokken started.

Litney interrupted him. "I asked the light about you. You don't have to do this. You can go back. And it sounds like you want to. You obviously know how serious this is, so maybe you should go."

"Grufwin said I had one chance to go back," Dokken told her. "I didn't take it."

"Well, I guess you get one more. Dokken, I want you to go back." When she saw him beginning to object, she hurried on. "No, now don't get mad, Dokken, that's not what I mean. I've been so thankful to have you here, but I don't want you to get hurt or, or worse. After all . . . like you said . . ."

"But you're going to do it?"

She nodded.

"Then I should—"

"But Dokken, I have the bracelet," Litney said. "It might give me some protection that you don't have."

Dokken's face flashed with red fear, but then it stilled, and he met Litney's eyes with calm certainty. "We started on this together, and we will finish it together."

"You know what could happen," Litney said staring directly into Dokken's eyes. "Are you sure?"

Dokken turned the question back on her, "Are you?"

"No," Litney said. "But I have to do it."

71

"So do I." Dokken stood and reached out a hand. Litney took it, and they stepped back onto the river bank. "Okay, so where would you like to go look for death?"

"Dokken," Litney said, trying for a tone of warning even as she laughed. "I don't know where to go or what to do. The light couldn't tell me."

"Should we sit here and wait for something to happen?"

"I have no reason for saying this, but I doubt Mala would come to the Rock. It seems to be a power opposite of hers."

Dokken thought of his science teacher droning on about magnets. "But don't opposites attract?"

"You're right. I don't know." Litney shrugged. "It's just for some reason I think we need to keep walking along the river."

"Then let's do it."

"MAYBE I WAS WRONG," A TIRED LITNEY said over her shoulder later. "It's horrible walking down here."

"Do you want me to lead? I think you're getting the worst of it having to push the weeds and branches out of the way all the time," Dokken offered.

Litney stopped and stretched her back. "Yeah, maybe I'll let you go in—" She screamed and disappeared.

"Litney!" Dokken shouted and looked all around him. She had been standing right in front of him. Where had she gone?

"Help!"

He saw something in the river. Dokken tried to run along the shore, but the branches and weeds felt like hands grabbing at him, slowing him down. He took his walking stick and began slicing at the growth in front of him. He could have sworn he saw the branches and weeds recoil when the stick touched them. This allowed him to move more quickly, but when he looked for Litney in the water, he still seemed to be losing ground.

Litney was doing her best to keep her head above the water. She was a strong swimmer, always had been, so why was she having such a hard time? Something was pulling her under. Was she stuck in a current? A whirlpool? The riverbank was changing, so that meant she had to be moving. Did whirlpools move?

The next time she was dragged under, Litney opened her eyes and looked at her feet. She saw something wrapped around her ankles. It couldn't be weeds, because she had already figured out she was moving. So what in the world was it? The water was dark enough toward the bottom that whatever it was stayed hidden.

Almost out of breath, she swam upward as hard as she could and gasped for air. A quick glance backward, and she saw Dokken's orange head as he was trying to follow her on the shore. He was getting farther away. "Something's got m—!" Under again. This time, she reached down to her ankles and felt, well, it felt like a slimy hand. Like a hand made out of fish's scales. She pulled herself into a crouching position, which was difficult because of the speed at which she was being carried, and squinted. She could just make out what looked like a fish, and by the looks of it, a huge one. But it was swimming upside down—she could see its white belly, glowing sickly in the dark water. Litney couldn't figure out why a fish would be swimming upside down, but then she saw that the fish had hands. When the fish saw that she had figured out what it was, it gave her a malevolent smile and swam faster. This was the first time Litney noticed its eyes—they were green.

Terrified, Litney shoved off the stomach of the fish and burst into air. With no time to get a full breath, she managed to hear Dokken shout,

73

"Knife!" before she was pulled under again. He sounded farther away than ever.

Of course—her knife. It was awkward with the water rushing about her, but she managed to reach into her backpack. It seemed like the knife threw itself into her hand, and she slashed down at the hands around her ankles. A loud roar filled the water as did a cloud of dark purple, and the grip on her ankles lessened. She gave one more hack with the knife and was free.

With one great kick, she made it to the surface. With two more, she was at a dead tree along the shore. She found the strength to pull herself out of the water and flop onto the shore.

Her breathing had almost returned to normal by the time Dokken reached her. "Are you okay?"

"Yeah. I think so."

"What happened?" Dokken asked.

"I was talking to you, and then suddenly I was in the water. I didn't fall. Something grabbed me and pulled me in." Both her voice and her body began to quiver.

"You were moving so fast."

"A fish with hands had a hold of me," Litney told him.

"A fish with hands?"

"Yeah," Litney said, pushing the wet hair out of her eyes. "And vivid green eyes."

Dokken's eyes went wide. "Do you think it was Mala?"

"Probably," Litney said. "You should have seen the look it gave me when I saw it. I don't even know how to describe it. Pure evil, but also some sort of crazy joy—as if nothing could have made it happier than killing me. It had the exact same green eyes as Mala and the dogs." She shivered harder. "Now that I think about it, the fish was holding me under for longer each time. I'm sure it enjoyed watching me struggle, seeing me afraid."

Dokken took off his backpack and handed her a blanket from inside. "You need this to warm up."

Litney put the blanket around her shoulders. "Thanks."

"Do you want any water? Do you need the first aid kit?" Dokken hadn't known what to do when he had seen her in the water. He had never liked to swim, and he had told himself that one of them needed to stay out of the water. Now though, he was feeling like he hadn't done enough to help her. Again.

"I've had plenty of water for a while, thanks." Litney checked the skin around her ankles. It was red, but there weren't any cuts. "I'll probably be bruised tomorrow, but I don't think I need anything from the first aid kit."

"I'm not a good swimmer," Dokken said lamely.

"Then it's a good thing you weren't in the water. I love to swim, and it took everything in me to get up to the surface and breathe."

"But . . . that's not what I mean." Dokken said, "I should have jumped in and tried to help you."

"If you're not a good swimmer, that would have been a stupid thing to do," Litney told him. "You probably would have drowned. Anyway, you were the one who saved me."

"Yeah, right." His expression turned morose.

As she watched him, Litney could see that he was feeling badly that he maybe hadn't helped her enough. She also suspected he was thinking he should have just gone home. She said, "I had completely forgotten about my knife until that last time when I surfaced and heard your yell. It was weird. When I reached in my backpack, it felt like the knife jumped into my hand, as if it had heard you as well and was eager to help. I cut the hands holding onto me. That's how I got free. So, thanks."

Dokken shrugged. He was relieved at least to see her shaking had begun to subside.

Litney was trying not to cry. "Here I'm supposed to go out and find Mala, but whenever I do, I almost get killed."

"Yeah, this fish . . . and those dogs certainly weren't inviting us to a tea party."

"So, how do we do this without dying?" Litney wanted to know.

"The light didn't say anything about that?"

"No."

Dokken shook his head. "I don't know, but how about we try getting away from the river for a while? Fighting the overgrowth is too tiring, and now it's become dangerous to stay down here. And, hey, why don't I lead for a little bit?"

"That sounds good to me." Litney handed the blanket back to Dokken.

"You sure you don't need it any more?"

"We keep forgetting these things are magic," Litney said, pointing to her now dry clothes.

"So, the knife probably did jump in your hand."

"Probably."

"You ready?" Dokken asked.

Litney nodded.

They found a path heading up the hill and into a forest of pine trees. The trees were pencil-straight, and the forest floor was clear of almost all brush. A carpet of orange needles spread out before them.

"Much better," Litney said.

"Much," Dokken agreed.

Away from the weeds of the river bank, Litney gladly followed Dokken for a while.

LITNEY BRUSHED AT HER NOSE. A seriously bad smell was growing. She glanced ahead at Dokken, who looked supremely unconcerned. *Boys,* thought Litney. Some of the boys in her class were always farting and laughing about it. It was disgusting. Finally, as yet another wave of foul odor reached her nose, she couldn't keep quiet any longer. "I hate to be rude, but do you need to go to the bathroom? Maybe that fish scared you more than you thought?"

"It isn't me," Dokken protested, wrinkling his nose at the horrible smell. "I thought it was you. I kept walking faster and faster, hoping the smell would stay behind me."

They both began to laugh.

"So, if it isn't me and it isn't you," Dokken said, "what stinks?"

Litney took a deep breath and coughed, but the rank odor changed just a bit, and she recognized it. "Oh, I know. That's a skunk. It smells like it is pretty close, too."

"Boy, skunks are nasty. I can't think of an animal I hate more."

"Have you ever smelled a skunk before, city boy?" Litney asked.

"No, but why do they have to stink so much? The world would be much better off if we got rid of all the skunks."

"Some of us might say the same thing about humans," said a little black and white animal standing in the middle of the path.

Both Dokken and Litney held their noses and blinked back tears. "Aw, man, can you just go on your way? You smell, and we aren't going to hurt you," Dokken said.

"Dokken," Litney's eyes warned that they didn't want to make this creature angry. "I'm sorry for my friend here. He's from the city so his poor nose is only used to the lovely smells of garbage and pollution."

The skunk smiled at this.

"I'm Litney."

Lifting its head and tail high, the skunk replied, "I am Sensho."

"I'm Dokken," but no one seemed to care.

"Not many humans understand us. How is it that you can?"

Litney held up her wrist.

"The bracelet helps you?" Sensho asked.

"You don't know about the bracelet?" Litney asked. "I thought everyone knew about it."

"We skunks keep to ourselves, so I haven't heard why the bracelet is so special."

"It's given to all the women in my family. It comes to us typically when we turn sixteen, but I'm only fourteen . . ." Litney sighed. "I'm not explaining this very well."

"She got the bracelet early because something evil brought her to this world, hoping to steal the bracelet," Dokken said succinctly.

"And now we have to find this evil and defeat it," Litney added.

"But if you meet evil, won't you get hurt?" Sensho asked.

"It sure would seem so." Litney told him about the fish, while Dokken told him about the dogs.

"Sounds like you two work well toge—" Sensho stopped and all three turned when they heard a crashing noise coming up the hill.

"What's that?" Dokken asked.

The strangest cry they had ever heard ripped through the air. It was like a blending of a growl, howl, and scream.

"Sensho, do you know what that is?"

The skunk rose onto his hind feet and said, "From the sounds of it, probably a bear."

"A bear?" Dokken's voice squeaked. "Seriously?"

"Seriously, yes. A seriously angry bear at that," Sensho qualified.

"What do we do?"

"It's coming fast. There isn't time for you to run. Stand behind me. Better yet, hide behind a tree. If I have to spray it, I will. Do you have anything you can cover your noses and eyes with? I won't spray you, but the mist from my tail can be painful enough."

Dokken whipped his backpack off and found two white handkerchiefs on top. He kept one for himself and handed the other one to Litney. "Here."

Each of them picked a different tree and put the cloths over their noses and mouths. Peering out, they watched Sensho, who looked like a very small sentinel protecting this part of the forest.

The cry rang out again, and this time it was followed by what sounded like sobs.

The creature must have crested the hill, because Sensho called out in a loud voice, "Bear, are you hurt?"

An enormous grizzly bear barreled toward Sensho, but even in her crazed state, the bear saw what it was she was about to attack. She veered to the left and stopped. The bear raised her head and screamed—there was no other way to describe the sound—and then started to huff. It took them awhile to realize the bear was saying something: "Dead, dead, dead."

"Who is dead?" Sensho inquired.

The bear answered with a low growl that grew into a shattering roar, then she collapsed to the ground.

Sensho dropped to all four paws, took two steps forward and repeated, "Are you hurt?"

Rolling violently this way and that, the bear shouted, "No!" She lumbered to her feet and reared, scraping huge claws down a tree. Bark gaped open as the bear did it again and again. The bark quickly reduced to shreds.

Sensho tried a different question. "Bear, what's your name?"

Falling to all fours, the bear answered, "Asta."

"I'm Sensho."

Litney thought about stepping out and introducing herself, but she didn't want to upset the bear again. She motioned to Dokken to stay quiet, and he nodded.

"Oh Sensho, Sensho."

"Yes, Asta."

"What am I going to do?"

"Maybe if you tell me what's happened, I can help you."

Asta began pacing back and forth. "Every mother bear can't wait to take her cub fishing for the first time. My son had been begging me to go for weeks, and I decided this morning we would go. I've never seen him so excited. He woke me up before it was light out and asked if it was time to go yet. I should have taken him then. Right then. But no, I had to tease him. I made him collect me some blackberries first. Enough to fill five maple leaves." The bear stopped and looked at the skunk.

"Joy and excitement come easily. Patience must be taught by someone who loves us," Sensho said.

The bear resumed her pacing. "When we finally got to the river, he took at least an hour trying to find the perfect spot for us to stand. We wandered upstream, down. We crossed. We crossed back. When he had found what he thought was the perfect spot, I made him move." Asta stopped moving and her voice cracked. "I told him I smelled humans there. It wasn't safe. He didn't cry, but I could see how disappointed he was." Asta looked at Sensho, as if waiting for Sensho to tell her how horrible a mother she was.

"Humans have a smell that all of us have come to fear," Sensho said with the slightest turn of his head in Dokken's direction. "It was wise of you to be concerned."

"We moved downstream. The spot Ta—" Asta's voice failed her again. She sobbed a moment, then continued. "The spot Tato picked, I worried it was too deep, but I had already said no once. How could I again? I sat up on the bank, and you should have seen how serious Tato was. His nose nearly in the water, his rump up in the air." Sensho waited, and even the forest was silent, as if everything and everyone waited to hear how Asta's story would end. "And then . . . and then he was gone."

"Where did he go?"

"I saw him in the water. I kept shouting at him to swim, swim! But he didn't. I heard him shout, 'I can't!' and then he went under. He came up once more and yelled, 'Something's got me.' I jumped in, I swam as hard as I could, but I couldn't catch up to him. He was moving too quickly."

Dokken and Litney exchanged uneasy glances. This sounded familiar.

"Finally, I saw him, up on the shore of a flat. He, he wasn't breath-ing. Or moving. He, he, he—" Asta reared again and hit a tree with the entire weight of her body. The tree cracked, but didn't fall. Needles show-ered down. Litney and Dokken covered their ears against her deafening cries and watched as Asta continued to hit the tree as hard as she could until it began a slow, crackling descent.

A few startled birds took to the air as the tree smashed to the ground.

When quiet had descended on the forest again, Sensho asked, "Do you know what happened to Tato?"

"I just stood there, nuzzling his little body, trying to get him to . . . to move. That's when I heard something behind me in the water. I turned and saw a fish. It was huge, longer than any bear I've ever known. I asked it if it knew what had happened. It said to me, 'I wanted to kill today. What I want-ed to kill got away. Your cub was the next thing I saw.'"

Litney stepped out from behind the tree. "Did the fish have hands?"

Asta reared at the sudden appearance of a human and snarled, revealing white sharp teeth. "Who are you?" she roared.

Sensho tried to calm the bear down. "This is Litney. She is the one who wears the bracelet." While that had meant nothing to Sensho minutes earlier, he hoped the bear would have heard about her.

"You . . . you are the one?"

"Yes." She held up her wrist with the bracelet to prove it. "We were talking with Sensho when you came up the hill. We hid—and so we heard your story. I'm sorry about what happened to your son."

"Me, too," Dokken said, revealing his hiding place. Asta growled at him and then she checked the other trees to see if any more humans were going to pop out.

"Did the fish have hands?" Litney repeated.

"A fish doesn't have hands. Are you stupid?" But then Asta thought for a moment. "I was so angry about Tato that I didn't realize, but yes. Yes, the fish had hands. It actually waved at me before it disappeared. How could you know that?"

"As . . . as my friend and I were walking this morning, a fish with hands grabbed me and pulled me down river."

"Then . . . then you're the one the fish wanted to kill. You! You should be dead! Not my Tato! It's your fault. It's all your fault!" Asta roared and readied herself for the attack.

"Stop!" Sensho shouted, turning his tail to face the bear. "I'll spray you if I have to. Look, hurting Litney isn't going to bring Tato back. You must know that."

The absolute anger in every fleck of her being took Asta several huge breaths to control. When she did, the sobbing returned. "He's dead. My baby's dead. Dead, dead, dead."

It didn't take Litney long to decide Asta was right—it was her fault. If she hadn't escaped, Tato wouldn't be dead.

Dokken whispered, "But then you would have been the one who was dead."

"How, how did you know what I was thinking?" Litney whispered back.

"I don't know." Dokken looked as startled as she felt. "I just could."

Litney knew now was not the time to discuss that, but she'd have to remember to ask Dokken more about it later.

The bear, deterred by Sensho's threat, moved back from them and sat down. She stared out into the forest, looking miserable.

Litney, Dokken, and Sensho said nothing. What was there to say? There was no way any of them could make it better.

The bracelet grew warm on Litney's arm—not the alarming hot when something bad was about to happen—but a prodding warm. Like the sun's gentle suggestion to take off one's coat on a warm day. Litney tried to ignore it. The last thing Asta needed or wanted was to talk to her.

But the bracelet would not be ignored.

Litney walked over to Asta, whose eyes focused and filled with anger.

"I wanted to kill you," the bear said. "I still want to kill you."

Litney nodded and managed not to back away. She said, "You're angry."

"There's no word for what I am."

Litney nodded again because she didn't know what else to do. She couldn't stand the intensity of the bear's stare, so she looked away and picked at her arm hairs.

"Tell me about the fish," Asta said.

"It's a being called Mala. We've seen it as a fish and as a dog. We're not sure what it is, but we do know it's evil."

Asta thought for a moment, then said, "I'll find and destroy this Mala."

"That's what I'm trying to do."

Asta laughed, but there was no humor in the sound. "Why are you trying to destroy Mala?"

"Because Mala wants the bracelet, and if she gets it, there's no telling what she might do."

"How are you, a human, and a small one at that, going to do that without dying?" Asta wanted to know.

"I don't know," Litney admitted.

"How are you going to do that without other innocent creatures dying?"

"I don't know." Litney said and sighed. "Look, it isn't like I asked to do this. I was . . . was chosen, and so I'm going to try and do the best I can. I can hardly stand the thought of what happened to your son, and I want nothing more than to quit and go home so no one else gets hurt. But I can't do that because if I do go home, then all sorts of creatures and people could get hurt. All sorts of creatures and people could feel as badly as you do. I have to stop Mala." By the time she was done speaking, Litney's eyes were huge and shining.

It was the first time Asta saw her as a child, just like Tato. Something in the bear relented. "I loved my son. I can't . . . I can't imagine life without him."

"I wish there was something—"

"I'll do what I can to protect you," the bear interrupted her to vow.

"What?" Litney was sure she had misheard the bear.

Now the bear took a deep breath, seeming to swell in both size and resolve. "I'll do what I can to protect you."

"But—"

"You're in danger from the one who killed my son. I'll do what I can to stop the same thing from happening to you, or to anyone else. I couldn't save my son because I wasn't prepared." Asta paused, and Litney guessed it was so she could regain control over her voice that had started to waver. After a moment, Asta cleared her throat and added, "Your mother can't do it for you because she isn't here. So I'll do it. It's the only thing that makes sense."

"Asta—"

"I'm certain about this. Please, don't deny me," the bear said.

There was so much pain and grief in Asta's eyes and voice that Litney had no choice but to answer, "I'm honored to have you by my side."

Dokken called, "Are you two okay?"

"Yes. We were just talking," Litney said, her hand on the bear's back as the two of them walked toward Dokken and Sensho. "Dokken, Asta has decided to travel with us."

"What?" the boy couldn't believe he had heard Litney right.

"Asta's going to do what she can to protect us."

"But—"

Litney gave him a warning glance. "And we are honored to have her."

Dokken read her expression. "Well, okay."

"Sensho," Litney said, turning to the skunk, "I can't promise you protection or safety, but I invite you to join us, too."

The little skunk stood quickly with delight, which sent a strong wave of odor all around. "I'm yours until you ask me to leave."

* 10 *

Field of Fire

AN IDEA WAS BEGINNING TO HATCH in Litney head. She asked Asta and Sensho, "Is there any place where creatures gather around here? It might be smart to go and listen to what they're saying. Maybe others have experienced Mala firsthand. We could get more of an idea of what we are dealing with."

The answer came quickly. "The Field of Fire. It's a busy place this time of year, and it's not far," Asta said. "We should be able to get there in a couple of hours."

The four of them set out with Asta in front while Sensho waited to take up the rear. "I'll save your nose," he teased Dokken with a wink.

"Hey, I never had the chance to apologize about that. I know what it's like to get teased for something you have no control over." Dokken pointed to his freckles and hair. "I'm sorry I was so rude. You're our friend, and, anyway, I must be getting used to you. You just smell like part of the forest now."

As they traveled Sensho wanted to learn more about the bracelet, so Litney told him how she had found it.

"It just appeared?" Sensho called from behind them.

"Yes."

"And there was a note from your very own mother inside?" the skunk asked.

"Yes. It's funny. When I first looked at the note, I thought the handwriting looked kind of familiar. I wondered if it had been written by one of my friends . . . now I realize that a part of me must have recognized my mother's handwriting. It's just that she had written it when she was younger, so it wasn't exactly the same."

"I wonder where the bracelet goes when the adventure is finished?" the skunk mused.

"I've wondered that, too." Litney rubbed the bracelet, and suddenly she couldn't imagine being without it. Just the thought of it being gone brought a stone to her stomach.

THEY HAD BEEN WALKING FOR ALMOST two hours when they heard a small thud, like a small stone hitting the trunk of a tree, followed by an "Ouch!" followed by another smaller thud. They went to investigate, but it took them awhile before they discovered a hummingbird laying on the ground, moaning. They all crowded around, their heads nearly touching, looking down at the little bird.

"Oh, my head," the hummingbird said. One wing seemed to hold its green head while the other was pressed to its ruby chest.

"Are you all right?" Litney asked. She had seen hummingbirds before as they feasted at her grandfather's feeders, but she had never seen one this close, nor had she seen one that wasn't zooming about on near-

ly invisible wings. Its beak was a little thicker than the needle her grandmother used for quilting, and its breast was bigger than she had expected.
The little birds looked much leaner in flight.

The bird suddenly seemed aware of the faces pressed together all
around it, and its tiny eyes went wide. It popped up onto its feet and tried
to take off, wings buzzing a few times before the bird flopped again onto
its back. "Don't hurt me," it said in a pathetic little voice. "Please, please
don't hurt me."

"We're not going to hurt you. I asked if you were hurt."

The bird must have decided Litney was telling the truth, because
it answered in its small high voice, "Not really. This happens all the time."

"What happens all the time?" Dokken asked.

"I run into things. These wings get going so fast I sometimes can't
see where I am or what's in my way until it's too late—then *wham! bam!*
I hit a tree. Or a barn. I even hit a fence post yesterday."

"I'm so sorry. I'm Litney, by the way."

"Hello, I'm Hummidramandaputalando, but," the hummingbird
said when he saw Litney's face, "you can call me Hummer."

"Oh, good. That I can handle. Here, let me help you." Litney
eased her fingers under the bird's back and scooped him up. Then she
tipped him up so his feet landed in her other hand. "Can you stand?"

"I think so. Who's everyone else?"

"I'm Dokken."

"Sensho . . . and that's Asta," the skunk said, introducing the
bear whose head and bulk filled half the circle of those looking at the little bird. She had started looking grief-struck again as she backed out of the
circle and walked a couple of steps away from everyone else.

"What's wrong—" Hummer started to ask, but Litney quickly
whispered to the bird what had happened. "Oh. That's terrible, that's hor-

rible, that's nasty." Hummer spoke as he tested his wings and managed to lift an inch off Litney's hand. "You have my greatest sympathies, Asta. We lost an egg from the nest this summer. One of my brothers. The wind came up so hard one day, it blew the egg right out of the nest. When the storm died down and Momma and Poppa had a chance to look for it, it had been smashed against a rock. We were so sad."

Asta growled a thanks for the sympathy.

"Are you feeling better?" Dokken asked Hummer.

"Well, I believe I am. There's only four of you now instead of eight," Hummer answered him, "so yes, I think I'm doing better. Where are you all going?"

"To the Field of Fire," Litney said. "Asta said it was something we needed to see."

"Wait a minute. Hold on there. Stop everything," all these came out of Hummer so rapidly, they sounded like gunfire. The bird continued, "Why exactly are two kids here in the forest talking to animals in the first place? My momma told me to stay away from people, that they don't understand us creatures. And to have two humans, a grizzly bear, and a skunk traveling together isn't something you see every day."

"Your mother is probably right about humans not spending much time with animals, but Litney has the bracelet," Dokken said.

"Really? *Really?*" The excitable little bird jumped and hummed but still couldn't quite fly for more than a second or two, even though its wings blurred with their fast beating. "Momma told me all about the bracelet. When I couldn't sleep at night, she used to tell me all sorts of stories about it. Is it true it can make you fly?"

"I don't think so," Litney laughed.

"Really?" Hummer asked, "Because in almost every story Momma tells me, the girl with the bracelet flies."

Litney looked at Dokken and shrugged. "Well, I don't know if it's possible. I haven't tried."

"Why wouldn't you have? Flying is amazing. Momma says, you have to try flying, even if it scares you to death."

With a smile, Dokken asked, "Does flying scare you?"

Hummer nodded. "Only a little now. It still hurts though."

"How long have you been flying?"

"Almost a week."

"Well, I'd say you're doing great. It must be hard flying in a forest with so many trees. Do you ever get to fly in a field? That might be easier," Litney suggested. "I know when I learned to ride my bike, my dad took me to a parking lot so I wouldn't hit anything."

"What's a parking lot?" Hummer asked.

"Oh, it's where we park our cars," Dokken said.

"What are cars?"

"Smashers," Sensho replied before the children could say anything.

Hummer's face took on a look of terror. "Momma's told me about smashers—they're bad, evil. They kill."

Litney blushed. "I suppose that's how an animal would see them. We use cars because they help us get places."

"I know you aren't blessed enough to have wings," Hummer said with pride and a whirr of wings, "but can't you walk?"

"We do walk, sometimes, though probably not as much as we should. It's just easier to drive a car."

"And faster," Dokken added.

"Sometimes faster isn't better," Hummer said, rubbing his head once more. "It can get you into trouble."

"Very true."

Dokken turned to Litney, "Can you fly?"

"I don't know."

"Let's see if you can," Dokken urged.

"Now probably isn't the time to try it," Sensho said, pointing to the trees, "as Hummer can testify."

"And I certainly don't want to try at the Field of Fire with everybody watching. Later." But it would be hard for her to wait. Litney had a recurring dream where she was being chased by something, she never knew what. And while that part of the dream terrified her, the other part made up for it. She would be running away from her pursuer and soon her feet would no longer be pounding on the ground. Instead, she'd be floating, flying, higher and higher until she could use one finger to push off the tree tops and shoot up into the bottoms of the clouds.

"Momma told me to meet her at the Field. She said if I was good today I could stay up a little late for the Song," Hummer said.

"What song?" Dokken asked.

"The Song of Silence."

Dokken said, "That doesn't make any sense. How can there be a song of silence?"

"That's what I thought, but wait and see. That's what Momma always says."

"Would you like me to carry you to the Field?" Litney asked.

Hummer lifted his tail feathers and plunked down on his little bottom. His tiny feet stuck out in front of him. He said almost royally, "Yes, please."

As the afternoon wore on, the five travelers walked steadily through the forest of solemn, straight trunks, their footfalls muffled by the thick layer of needles. Though a few slices of sun cut through the gloom now and again, they walked mostly in a kind of green twilight. Few animals lived in this sterile environment, so they didn't hear too many birds or see much skittering among the roots of the pines. Finally, they came to an opening in the forest, and the slanting evening sun washed brightly over a wide meadow of grasses and wild flowers. Though Litney and Dokken already knew they had found the Field, Asta announced that they had arrived. Hummer, who was feeling much better, said he had better be off to find his mother. "Thanks again!" he called, zigzagging off.

"It's a good thing there aren't many trees around here," Sensho said, watching the little bird narrowly miss hitting a wolf in the back of the head.

"Wow," Dokken said. "Look." Nearly every manner of being was arriving at the Field—creatures with wings, creatures with any number of legs (and some with none at all), creatures who crawled, waddled, walked, slithered or flew. "Look at him," Dokken pointed to a huge buck deer whose antlers were so big, Dokken didn't know how he could keep his head up.

"And the fireflies," Litney whispered. "It looks like half a good night's stars have fallen." The edges of the Field, places surrounded by the dimness of the forest, were lined with flickering light.

"Let's sit over here," Asta said. She led them to a spot on a grassy rise and they sat down next to a family of otters. The three kits wrestling in the grass stopped so suddenly when the humans appeared that the one perched on his sister's legs fell over.

"Mommy! Mommy!" all three called in unison. "Mommy, there are stinky humans here!"

"Shh," the mother otter said with an embarrassed smile. "Not all humans are stinky."

"But you said—"

"Shh," and this time the kits must have realized their mother was serious, because they said nothing more. The mother otter turned to the newcomers, looking just a little embarrassed. "I'm Watanwa, and this is my mate, Trituno. My rather loud-mouthed children are Popo, Infina, and Quatar."

"Hi, I'm Litney. This is Dokken, Sensho, and Asta."

The father otter, Trituno, leaned closer. "How is it two young humans are here among us?"

Litney held out her wrist. "I have the bracelet."

Watanwa gasped and stared at it. "You are the one? I've heard of you all my life. I never imagined . . . Trituno, did you hear?"

"Since I'm right here, yes, I did."

Watanwa gave her husband a little swat, and he wrestled her to the ground for what looked like a kiss. "Trituno! You are as bad as the children."

"I'll take that as a compliment," he said, letting his mate up. He approached Litney and gave a bow. "It's wonderful to meet you."

"Thank you. Do you mind if we share this spot with you and your family?"

Trituno bowed. "It would be an honor indeed."

As soon as Litney and Dokken sat down, the three kits were on them, their tiny bodies feeling like a cross between a cat's soft fur and a snake's sinuous movements.

"You have the bracelet?" "You sure do smell funny." "Did you come with the bear and the skunk?" The questions came fast and furious with no real opportunity for Litney to answer. She couldn't get a word in. "Watch what I can do." With this, one of them (Litney couldn't tell them apart) wrapped itself into the shape of a doughnut and rolled down the hill.

"Ooh, my turn. Watch me!"

"I'm next. Let me go."

Before long, the three of them tussled, and while Litney saw a flash of teeth now and then, no one seemed to be hurting another.

"That's the reason we sit in the back," Watanwa said, but with a smile.

The kits unwound themselves from one another and dashed back up to the top of the hill. This time it was Sensho's turn to be investigated. "You're a skunk, aren't you?"

"Yes, I am." He tensed.

"Sometimes we call Popo a skunk because he can make his bottom smell—"

"Quatar! Get over here right now," his mother demanded.

The little brown body slithered across the grass and sat by his mother. "Do we talk like that?" she asked him sternly.

"Not when you can hear," the otter answered honestly.

His mother had a hard time not laughing. "Quatar," Watanwa said warningly.

The little kit sighed. "Mommy, I wasn't saying Mr. Sensho smelled. I was saying Popo smelled. I don't think Mr. Sensho smells really at all."

"Why thank you, Quatar," the skunk said.

"Popo does smell sometimes, Mommy," Quatar confided.

"Quatar!"

"Sorry."

"Now go off and play." Watanwa turned to Sensho. "Sorry about that."

"Not at all. It's wonderful that anyone smells more than I do."

LITNEY AND DOKKEN NOTICED THAT MANY of the animals would look at them, then turn to their neighbors. A low buzz and growl and hum of conversation circled the Field. Some pointed to Litney. "I think we're getting talked about," Dokken said.

Litney nodded. "I'm just glad no one is being scared off because of us, though. Many animals are scared of people."

"I think they're about ready to begin," Trituno said to the two of them. "Kits, come here and sit by your mother and me."

The three little otters dashed to their parents, and Litney and Dokken were surprised at how still they suddenly were. When Trituno noticed their surprise, he whispered, "The only other time besides the Song of Silence where they are this quiet is when they are sleeping."

The milling in the Field began to settle, and Litney saw that night had spread itself around them. The fireflies no longer held to the edge of the Field, but flew among the many other animals, their flickering little lights mimicking the stars popping out in the darkening sky. Her parents would have called the night romantic; Litney thought it magical—and she didn't throw that word around now as easily as she had before she had received the bracelet. The darkness had a feel to it, as if something, or someone, had arrived.

A moose, with antlers that looked like petrified tree limbs, walked slowly into the middle of the field, its stride and carriage weighty with drama. His legs were surprisingly thin for how big and heavy his body looked, but he walked with dignity. He snorted. "This Field is a place where we forget, for the moment, about eating or being eaten. In this place, we find peace only if we have peace."

This quieted down the last of the animals who were moving around. The moose continued, "We welcome any who are new this evening. If you are uncertain about what to do, do what everyone else is doing." Litney guessed the sounds she heard were laughter. "As usual, the crickets will begin. Then the fireflies, then comes the Song of Silence. Let us begin." With that the moose walked toward the hill where Dokken and Litney sat with the others. He stood to the side of the hill, right next to where Litney was sitting, so close she could feel his warmth, hear his breath.

Because of that, it took her a moment to realize a lone cricket had started a beat. *Chirp. Chirp. Chirp.* Silence. *Chirp. Chirp. Chirp.* Silence. This time another joined in. *Chiiiirrrp. Chiiiirrrp.* Then another. *Chirrrppyy Chirp. Chirrrrppyy Chirp.* Soon a multitude of rhythms and pitches permeated the night and created a gentle rising and falling sensation, almost as if the earth were breathing. It reminded Litney of the jazz her parents listened to—beautiful, intense and slightly unsettling because one never knew what was going to coming next.

"Listen," Dokken whispered.

"I am." Litney sounded annoyed.

"No, listen."

It took her a moment, but then, under the rhythm, she heard the words. She couldn't catch them all, but phrases emerged . . . *the one who has come . . . what she must fight . . . the end is not clear . . . to rise one must fall . . . the answer is . . . listen . . . .* After that the words stopped, and one by one, the crickets stopped until all that could be heard was the lone *Chirp. Chirp. Chirp.*

Silence.

More silence.

Litney snuck a look at the moose, wondering if he had gotten it wrong. Maybe it went crickets, Song of Silence, then fireflies.

When she was about to ask Sensho what was happening, one firefly, directly across from the hill where they were sitting, lit and went dark. Lit and went dark. Two fireflies on either side joined it. Light. Dark. Light. Dark. Two more joined in and the pattern continued until a ring of flashing light surrounded the entire field.

Light. Dark.

Light. Dark.

Soon, Litney noticed the lights seemed to be moving toward the center of the field.

Light. Dark.

Closer.

Light. Dark.

It wasn't long before the fireflies converged in the middle and created a sphere of light. Then dark. Light. Then dark. The sphere of light began to swirl and spin, pulsate with movement and light. When the fireflies lit up, their combined fire was bright enough to illuminate the faces below them in the field. Those lucky creatures were bathed in the cool glow for but a moment before they disappeared.

Now the pace of light and dark quickened, faster and faster, until the light strobed in the dark night like applause. The tumbling mass of light flashed and flashed, flared and held for several seconds. Then all went completely dark.

Litney heard Dokken release his breath, and she realized she, too, had been holding hers.

In all her life, Litney had never experienced a silence like the one that followed. An absolute lack of sound. No cars or airplanes. No humming lights or machines. No voices. Nothing. It was so quiet, she could have sworn she heard the sound her eyelids made as they closed and opened. She strained to hear Dokken's breath again, or the moose's, but could not.

She found herself focusing on other things—the weight of her tongue in her mouth, the feel of her toes pressing one against the other.

When she looked down at her left hand, Litney realized it was dark and cold. All she could think was that it felt like night. Her skin even had a pale glow to it, moon-like, and her fingers, the tips of her fingers, sparkled like five stars. Her right hand was just the opposite—all warmth and light, it was bright enough that when she looked at it, she had to squint.

Sitting cross legged, she gazed at her left knee. It sharpened, hardened, turned jagged and rough—a mountain peak with a tree-line and a gentle fog around its summit. Her right knee smoothed and shimmered—a river with a deep bend. Chin to her chest she watched her heart's center opening into a vast darkness. She could not begin to count the number of universes she found there. She saw one star grow white bright, flare, then disappear. A hole appeared and swallowed four stars before disappearing again. After a while, everything came rushing together only to explode apart. Now another star brightened and enlarged, but this one seemed to be moving outside of her, hovering in front of her. She saw a face, no, thousands of faces within the star.

Hello, Litney, the voices sang, and Litney had never heard anything like it before—the sound their voices made was rain and sun, thunder and flower all combined.

Hello.

Do you know who we are?

Her eyes went to her wrist and then back to the star. *The ones who created the bracelet?*

Yes.

It is beautiful. You are beautiful.

Thank you. And thank you for taking the bracelet.

Will everything be okay?

You are not ready.

Litney felt the cold in her left hand shoot up her arm. *Do you want me to give it back? To find someone else?*

No, you are not ready to know if everything will be okay.

The cold receded. *I want to ask . . . I want to ask you what I should do or know or . . .*

Your heart and the bracelet will tell you what you need to know and do. Believe in them. The light diminished.

O-okay. Can't you tell me any more? Please?

Good-bye, Litney. The light moved back into her heart's universe.

Good-bye. Thank you, she called.

* 11 *

The Hiding Tree

EVERYONE AROUND HER WAS MOVING.

"Litney?" Dokken asked, touching her shoulder. "You okay?"

She looked at her arms and legs which were back to normal. Nothing was different. Except for maybe the leftover feelings she had—as if her body was full of everything and nothing all at once. "Yeah, I am."

"Litney." It was Trituno. "We are honored to have met you."

"Likewise. You have a wonderful family," she told him.

Watanwa came forward and put a paw on one of Litney's knees. "There are many stories about the bracelet. Some are funny—"

"Like the one where it turned the entire world purple for three days," Quatar said. "I love that one."

Watanwa smiled. "Yes, some are funny and some—"

"Are scary," Popo said, his little body shivering. "Like the one where Night grew so strong it wouldn't let the Sun rise any more. Dark. Lots of dark."

Sighing, Watanwa finished. "Funny, scary and—" She looked at her daughter.

Infina supplied, "Beautiful. Like the one where every time someone says something nice, a flower grows out of their mouth."

"We know that many of them are not true, but," and Watanwa spoke more quietly now and nudged Litney to stand and move away from everyone else. "But there is power in the bracelet. And there have been rumors going around about one who would do anything to get it."

"Do you mean Mala?"

"I don't know what this power is called."

Litney had been so caught up in what had happened to her at the Field that she had forgotten they had come wanting to gather information. Now was her chance. "I have met this power two times now. She told me her name was Mala. Do you know anything about her?"

"Before you arrived, I heard some of the creatures talking."

Eager, Litney asked, "What did they say?"

"She comes from three worlds away, and her powers here are already very strong. If she gets into your world, there's no telling what she could do," Watanwa warned.

"Has anyone noticed any weakness she might have?"

"No," Watanwa shook her head. "Because everyone's trying to stay as far away from her as possible." Her eyes went to her own children, as if checking to make sure they were all still there. "And some are saying that she has pulled people over to her side, which means you have to be careful who you trust. You never know who might be working for her."

Trituno appeared and said, "We'd better go. Popo and Quatar are fighting."

Watanwa sighed but with a smile. She said to Litney, "I wish we had more time to talk. Just be careful."

"We will." Litney gave the sinewy little animal a hug. "Thanks. Good bye!" she called, waving to the five otters as they tumbled, raced and slunk off toward the river. Her hand came to rest on her stomach, a gesture she wasn't aware she did whenever she got nervous.

"Wasn't that awesome?" Dokken asked when they were alone.

It took her a moment to answer. "The Song of Silence? Yes, it was amazing. What was it like for you?"

"You can't imagine how quiet it was."

She gave him a look.

"Okay, you can, but you can't imagine how quiet it was for *me*. Living in the city, there's noise all the time. I mean, there isn't a time of day or night when there isn't noise. You hear the person living above you, the family below, someone yelling outside, a car, a horn, sirens. Noise. This, this was something else."

"Did anything . . . happen to you during the Song?" Litney had to know.

"Mostly it was dark, but a few images did come. Or surface. It's hard to know what word to use. After I saw them or felt them or whatever, then they disappeared back into the darkness. I'm not sure how to explain it."

"What did you see?"

"I saw fire, the same color as my hair. And I saw water. The water started pushing down on the fire, and I remember feeling afraid. I didn't want the fire to go out. At the same time, I felt stronger and lighter than I ever have. The more the fire died down, the more powerful I felt. Finally, the fire completely disappeared, and then all I could hear was a rushing sound. It was dark for a while, and then I saw the sun rise and set really fast, probably twenty or thirty times, like the earth was spinning way, way faster. And then I was standing under a blue sky. But it wasn't in the city. It was some place else. A small town, maybe. There was a lot of sky. I remember the sky. Isn't that weird?"

"I wonder what it means?"

"Is it supposed to mean something?" Dokken seemed perplexed.

"I don't know, but that seems pretty . . . loaded."

"What was it like for you?" Dokken wanted to know.

"Like you said, it's hard to explain. My left hand was the night, my right hand the sun. One knee was a mountain, the other a river. And at my heart were all the universes in the . . ." she paused. Not in the world, not in the universe. "All the universes in creation."

Dokken's eyes had grown large. "Cool!"

"And one star grew and floated out of me and talked to me."

"Really?" Dokken asked.

"Only it wasn't just a star." Litney's eyebrows bunched as she tried to think of how to describe what she had seen. "It was all the people or creatures or whatever *within* the star. I think they were the ones who created the bracelet."

"What did they say?"

"That my heart and the bracelet would know what to do."

"Cool!" Dokken repeated.

"Have you two seen Asta?" Sensho asked, climbing the hill.

Both of them looked around. "No."

"I think she left after the fireflies," Sensho said. "She might have been afraid she wouldn't be able to listen to the Song."

The images Litney had seen had been powerful enough that she could believe that. "Why don't you both stay here. I'll go find her."

The only answer she got was Dokken's question to Sensho: "So what did you see?"

Litney guessed Asta would have slipped into the woods behind the hill since they were dark and quiet. It was the place she would have gone if she had wanted, needed some time alone.

Most of the animals had departed from the field, although a few still darted past her, alarmed by the strange human wandering in the woods. As Litney plunged deeper into the trees, she realized that if she had done this before, she would have been terrified. She would have been afraid of the bugs zinging by her head, not to begin to mention what animal was waiting to get her. But at some point during all of this, things had changed. She had changed.

Litney couldn't see much, although her bracelet was glowing enough that she didn't have to worry about tripping or running into things. "Asta?" she called quietly. "The Song is finished."

No answer.

Litney thought about calling out again but decided against it. After what had happened, Asta needed space. And time. Litney found a tree and sat down with her back against it. She was tired, but that wasn't surprising after all that had happened this long day. As she sat and listened to the quieting forest, she realized she felt more than tired. The insides of her body felt like they were being dragged down. She just didn't feel right.

She rubbed at her wrist and yawned. "Asta will find me when she's ready."

Litney fell asleep to the hoot of an owl, the buzz of a June bug.

The night, for the most part, gave itself over to peace.

LITNEY JUMPED AWAKE TO THE SOUND of snarling and growling. She stood up so fast that her back scraped up the bark of the tree. She put a hand to her head because she felt like she was going to faint. "Must've stood too quickly," she said.

When her mind had focused again, she realized that the sounds weren't coming any closer but neither were they moving away. Litney trained her bracelet on the ruckus: the growling, grunting and slamming together of bodies. One was a bear. She couldn't make out what the other was.

Fur and weight. Muscle and rage. Litney wanted to help, but she didn't know what to do. Eyeing the area around her, she found a stick that was about the size of a bat. She grabbed it and inched closer to the roiling mass.

"Litney, stay back!" Asta called out when she saw the girl.

"I want to help."

The creature wrestling with Asta lunged toward the sound of Litney's voice, but Asta gripped it tightly in a crushing bear hug. Litney tried to get a good look at it, but it was dark and the thing was moving around so much that she couldn't tell exactly what it was. For some reason, that frightened her.

Litney didn't know what to do, but she knew she had to something because she could see Asta's grip was weakening. The creature was obviously too strong for her to hit with the bat, so Litney dropped it. The voices from the star sounded in her head—*The bracelet will know what to do.* She pointed the bracelet directly at the creature. All that happened was that she saw that its eyes were green, and she got a rather close view of its gaping jaws.

Now what was she supposed to do?

Asta's paws slipped, and the creature lunged, but the bear managed to get another hold on it before it could get to Litney. Knowing Asta's hold wouldn't be able to last much longer and feeling as if she didn't have any other choice, Litney screamed and charged at the creature, head on. She held out the bracelet and closed her eyes at the exact moment that the bracelet grazed the creature's nose. Litney crumbled in fear as a horrible scream tore through the night. She was afraid it was her own. Her last.

But as the echoes died (and she was still alive), the forest returned to its former quiet. Which is why she had to ask Asta, "What happened? What was that? Was it Mala? Where did it go?"

"I don't know what it was," the bear huffed, her large body sinking to the ground in exhaustion. "It wasn't like anything I'd ever seen before. It was strong as a bear, quick as a wolf with teeth like a lion's. I don't know." The bear sounded exhausted.

Litney searched the ground for some hint of the creature's existence. Since the creature had had green eyes, Litney hoped that meant it was Mala and that she had just managed to defeat her. Somehow, though, she doubted it. Since there was nothing anywhere to indicate that there had ever been anything there, she asked, "Where did it go?"

"When the bracelet touched it, it was as if lightning shredded its body," Asta said. "One minute I was holding it, the next it exploded into light and was gone."

Litney crawled over to the bear and leaned against her. "Thank you for saving me."

"You saved yourself. You're a strong girl."

"But I was sleeping," Litney said, itching her arm, which had gone all tingly. She assumed it had to do with the explosion of light. "It could have attacked and, and killed me, and I would have never known. Thank you."

The bear put a paw on the girl's leg. "You're welcome."

"Darnit," Litney said.

"What's wrong?" Asta asked.

"My wrist. It's itching like crazy." Litney was scratching so hard she began to break the skin.

"You'd better stop. You're making yourself bleed," Asta told her.

"I can't stop. I've had poison ivy and the chicken pox, but nothing has ever itched like this. And it's getting worse." Her voice sounded odd.

Asta waited a minute or two, hoping it would pass. When it didn't, the bear put a paw on the girl's hand, "Litney, you've got to stop."

"Don't touch me!" Litney screamed. "Don't! It itches. I have to scratch it. I have to."

"What's going on?" Dokken asked as he and Sensho appeared.

"Make it stop. Please, make it stop!" Litney shouted.

"Her wrist itches," Asta explained, her voice concerned.

"Try not to itch it," Sensho offered. "Itching usually makes it worse—"

"Shut up!" Litney screamed. "You don't know what it's like. I have to make it stop." She began to take the bracelet off.

"Stop, Litney," Dokken said kneeling beside her and grabbing her arm. "You can't take the bracelet off."

"I have to. I HAVE TO!" Litney shoved at Dokken, trying to make him let go. "Let me take it off."

Dokken put Litney's arm underneath his elbow so she couldn't get at her wrist, and she couldn't get away. In the bracelet's faint glow, Dokken looked at her arm. He wasn't sure, but he thought he could see two different kinds of red streaks on her skin. The one set was obviously from her fingernails. The other, though, seemed to be beneath the skin, like veins and this second set was growing. They were climbing up her arm toward her shoulder.

"It's getting worse," Litney cried. "Now it's moving up my arm. I have to make it stop. You've got to let me make it stop. Just let me take the bracelet off." Litney pleaded as she began to struggle with Dokken.

Dokken could see by Litney's eyes that she was hysterical. She was beyond control. "Asta, you've got to help me."

The fatigued bear moved as fast as she could and sat on Litney's left arm, the arm without the bracelet. "Litney, I know it itches, but you have to stop."

"I can't," the girl sobbed. "Make it go away. It has to stop."

"What do we do?" Sensho asked.

Dokken looked at Litney's arm again. It was hard to tell with such poor light, but it almost looked like there were things crawling inside her skin. "Sensho, look at this," Dokken said.

The skunk brought his face right next to the girl's arm and asked, "Is there something in there?"

"That's what I was thinking. But how could something have gotten in there?"

Litney moaned.

Asta answered, "A creature tried to attack her. I managed to hold onto it, but Litney hit it with the bracelet and the creature exploded. Maybe some of it got into her?"

"Maybe. Wait a minute." Dokken peered at Litney's arm again. "Look." Both Asta and Sensho looked at the place where Dokken was pointing. "One of Mala's dogs bit her there yesterday. You can see the teeth marks—and look at how red they are. I'll bet that dog put something into her bloodstream. I'll bet it knew that it would itch, and she would want to take the bracelet off."

"What happens if she takes the bracelet off?" Sensho asked.

"We don't know for sure, but her mother told her she couldn't take it off for any reason until all of this was over."

"So, what do we do?" Sensho repeated as Litney's sobs grew louder.

"Is she okay?" Dokken asked Sensho. He held onto Litney's arm, fearfully watching as the redness crawled up her arm.

The skunk felt Litney's forehead. "She's feverish. You've got to hurry, Asta."

The bear growled in answer. She had taken matters into her own hands—or mouth, actually—and gripped the young girl's arm with her teeth. She bit Litney in the same place where the dog had bitten her and was trying to suck out whatever was under her skin.

Litney moaned. Her eyes opened, and she looked at her arm and Asta's big white teeth. She screamed. "Get off! Quit biting me. I thought you were my friend! Help! Help!" Litney strained as hard as she could against the hands holding her until her eyes rolled back in her head and she passed out again.

"Thank God," Dokken said. "I wasn't going to be able to hold her much longer."

"Me either," said Sensho, who had taken over control of the other arm.

"I've got one," Asta told them.

Sensho reached between the bear's teeth and pulled out a long green slimy thing. "Goodness. It looks like a slug," the skunk said.

"What's a slug?" Dokken asked, still not looking.

"A snail without a shell."

"Ewww," Dokken said, sneaking a peek. "That thing was in her?"

"Yes, and there's still one more to get," Sensho said. "Keep it up, Asta."

"I worry I'm hurting her," the bear mumbled, since her mouth was locked on Litney's arm.

"I'm afraid you have to," Sensho said. "You have to get it out. Who knows what it'll do if you don't."

It took several very long minutes of slurpy sucking, but finally, Asta got the second one out.

Dokken hadn't watched the process, but he was more than happy to hear the *squish* the creatures made when he stepped on them. "That's what you get for hurting her," he said. Then he asked, "Do you think she'll be okay?"

"I don't know," Asta said as she watched Sensho apply moss to Litney's arm to stop it from bleeding.

WHEN LITNEY CAME AROUND, SHE NOTICED that they were back in the Field. Near midnight, the moon's yellow light was rich and beautiful. It was bright enough for her to see her friends. She sat up and looked at Dokken, Sensho, and Asta. They were all looking at her intently. She asked, "What happened?"

"You fell asleep after the Song," Dokken said.

"Really?" Litney asked, rubbing her forehead. "But I remember getting up and talking to you, Dokken."

"You did, but then when you went into the forest to find Asta, and you fell asleep."

Litney seemed to remember that. "Right, but then I remember being woken up by something. By fighting. Asta, you were fighting a creature. A weird creature."

"Yes," Asta said, but she was having a hard time maintaining eye contact with the girl.

"I had to attack it with the bracelet. And then, and then something else happened." Absent-mindedly, she rubbed her arm. "But I can't remember." Litney looked at the three of them. "What was it?"

"Remember when you got bit by the dog?" Dokken asked.

"Yes. It bled, but it didn't hurt much. Why?"

"The dog put something in you," Dokken said.

"What was it?" Litney wanted to know.

"You don't want to know," Dokken replied. "Trust me."

"No, I do want to know," Litney said.

This time it was Sensho who spoke. "Sometimes the answer is worse than the question."

"Still, I have a right to know."

"Green slug things," Dokken said.

"Green slug things?" Litney repeated. "In my arm? Gross." Her body shuddered.

"Told you the answer was worse than the question," Sensho said under his breath.

"I remember itching," Litney said. "It was horrible. It wouldn't stop."

"You were going crazy," Asta said. "We had to get them out of you."

"How did you do that?" Litney asked.

No one answered.

"How did you do that?" she demanded again. "Wait. I remember. I woke up once and thought you were attacking my arm," she said to the bear. "You were sucking them out of me?"

Asta nodded. "I had to bite into the place the dog had bitten."

Litney shuddered again.

"We need some sleep," Dokken changed the subject, and pointing to his backpack, he said, "We have our tent."

"Yes, but I don't think we want to set that up in the middle of the Field," Asta said.

"I agree," Sensho said. "From all that's happened tonight, it's obviously too dangerous to be out in the open."

"What can we do, then?" Litney asked. "All of us are exhausted. We need sleep."

Asta said, "Some in my family have talked about a hiding tree around here. It has an ancient spell on it. Most animals don't know anything about it, but my great-great-grandmother learned about it, and she taught us to use it when hunters come around."

"But can you find it in the dark?" After everything that had happened, Dokken suddenly felt exhausted. He wasn't sure how much further his legs would be able to go.

"I don't think it's very far," Asta repeated. "Not far at all."

"Good," Dokken said, following Asta into the forest on a path that veered away from where Asta and Litney had been attacked.

"Not far at all."

"You already said that," Dokken told her.

"And I meant it. Here we are."

"Really? Really?"

Asta pointed her snout to a tree in front of them. The only thing distinguishing it from the flaky-barked pines around them was that it had no bark, so the tree looked like it had skin—white skin that glowed in the moonlight. Also unlike the soldier-straight pines, this tree's trunk bent and curved, its wide branches twisting upward.

Litney pointed the bracelet light at the tree and said, "Um, Asta, are you sure?" At eye level, the tree looked about as thick around as her father's leg. She saw a dark hollow near the ground that looked like a hole. "That's hardly big enough for Sensho to get in. There's no way you and Dokken and I are fitting in there."

"Have you learned nothing, child? Everything is more than it seems. Now I need to remember the spell." When Asta spoke, it was in a soft voice:

> Tree of light in a dark world,
> shelter the unsheltered,
> protect the unprotected.
> For a night give peace.
> For the day give strength.

"That was beautiful," Dokken said, "but I'm with Litney. I don't see how you are going to fit—"

Asta was gone. One minute she had been there, right in front of them. The next . . . where could she have gone? "Asta? Asta?" When there was no answer, Litney turned to Sensho. "Where did she go?"

"Let me see." The skunk walked to the tree. Then disappeared.

"How? How are they doing that?"

"Maybe if we walk toward it, the same thing will happen to us," Litney offered.

"What if it's—?"

"We aren't going to know unless we do it. So, here goes."

When Dokken stood alone in the forest, he had no choice but to follow.

"LOOK OUT!" LITNEY YELLED AS SHE GRABBED Dokken and pulled him close as a creature scuttled past them.

"That was . . . that was . . . but that couldn't have been—"

"Yes," Litney said, "That was an ant."

"What kind of ant grows taller than I am?" Dokken asked loudly so he could be heard over the noise inside the tree.

"We've shrunk."

He was about to disagree with her, but then he saw Sensho standing on what he knew was a snail shell but looked like a small boulder. When he looked around further, he saw hundreds of small glowing mushrooms that cast a dim light over the thousands, no probably millions, of ants moving around them. Since they were ants, Dokken was surprised their footsteps echoed throughout the tree. The *boom, boom, boom* shook the ground and his body. At first glance Dokken thought they were surrounded by pure chaos, but then he began to see patterns in their movement. He saw six major columns of ants climbing up the walls while four climbed down. Behind Asta several thousand ants seemed to congregate around something with more coming all the time. In front of him was what looked to be a major thoroughfare. Ants marched past them, not rushing, but very very determinedly.

"Sensho thinks this is like one of our freeways," Litney had to yell to be heard.

"So, what do we do? I mean, the good news is I doubt Mala could find us in here, but I can't sleep next to a freeway."

"I thought you were from New York City? I thought you could sleep next to anything," Litney teased. She turned to Asta and Sensho, "Any ideas?"

"This group behind us isn't moving. We could ask one of them for directions."

"Let's go," Litney said.

The four of them approached the fringe of the circle. "Excuse me," Litney said politely. "Could you tell us—"

An ant felt her with its antennae. Without warning that ant and the one next to it moved their thick hairy abdomens together and would have crushed her if she hadn't jumped back.

"Well," huffed Litney, breathing hard and pulling a piece of her hair out of her mouth. "They could have just said they were busy."

"Let me try," Dokken offered.

His efforts landed him in the dirt.

"I'm tired. I just want to sleep," Litney said, her voice wavering with the disappointment and frustration they were all feeling.

A female voice behind them said, "Greetings and welcome."

They turned to find an ant with wings and a crown standing before them. The continual noise of the footsteps had made it impossible to hear her approach. "I am Natta, Queen of the Tree of Hiding."

"Hello. I'm Litney."

The others introduced themselves.

"You wear the bracelet."

"Yes."

"There is much we need to talk about."

"Queen Natta, I would love to talk with you, but my friends need rest. They have had a long day."

"Of course, of course. You all need rest." She made a clicking noise and several of the ants streaming past them on the highway broke away and came toward them. "Please show our guests to the Chamber of Light."

Dokken looked at Litney who didn't want to say anything, but who also knew how important it was that they all get some rest. "I beg your pardon, Queen Natta, the Chamber of Light sounds lovely, and I can't wait to see it in the morning, but if we could just find a quiet and dark place to sleep."

"You need the Chamber of Light." The queen waited for Litney to object, and when she didn't, the queen smiled. "You are learning, little one."

"Why do you say that?"

"Your first request was for your friends. You also stood up for them when it seemed as if I had ignored you. But then, you yielded to my authority. Since this is my kingdom, it was right and good for you to do so. You may put your heart at ease. The Chamber of Light is where you go to sleep and to have all of the day's burdens removed from you. All that was wrong and heavy and hard is lifted from you. But only for the night. In the morning, all of your difficulties will return, but you will be completely refreshed, stronger and more able to handle them."

Litney's eyes were dangerously close to tears as she bent down on one knee. "Thank you, Queen Natta. That is exactly what we need."

The queen took one of her six legs and lifted Litney's chin up, "We all must work together right now. There is much to overcome. Come see me in the morning when you wake." Her wings came up, and she flew away with a *whirr*.

The four of them followed the ants, who led them to a hole in the ground. A path wound down, lit by more of the ghostly mushrooms. The farther down they went, the less they could hear the constant marching of the ant highway.

When their feet were the only things making noise, the path opened up into a large room that had things stuck to the wall.

"What are those?" Dokken asked.

"They look like milkweed pods. I used to love going out in the fields at my grandparents' farm and finding them. When you open them up, they have the softest, silkiest seeds inside." Litney stopped talking when an ant took her by the arm and led her to one of the pods. When the ant opened it up, she saw she had been right. Inside was the same silk she remembered. "This is where we sleep?" she asked.

The ant nodded.

Even though she was the size of an ant, it looked awfully small. Tight. She wasn't claustrophobic, but she didn't think she wanted to get in that pod and have the lid pushed down on her. Then she remembered Queen Natta's words. "Okay. I'll get in."

Asta and Sensho were used to hibernating in close spaces, so neither of them hesitated to climb into their pods. Dokken was so tired he was grateful for any place to lie down.

Before the lids were pushed down, Litney said, "Good night. Sleep tight."

* 12 *

Discovering

*L*ITNEY'S EYES OPENED SLOWLY. She didn't know how long she had been asleep because it felt like she had closed her eyes only seconds before but at the same time she felt completely recharged and refreshed. Pushing at the top of her pod, she peeked out. All the other pods were empty. *Oh no! How long have I slept?* she wondered, jumping to the floor. Her legs, which had been achy and rubbery when she had fallen asleep, now felt sure and strong. Her eyes were no longer gritty and sore. Even her arm, where Asta had sucked the slugs out, felt good.

Quickly, she began climbing up the winding path they had traveled down the night before. When she came out of the hole, she worried that something was wrong. She didn't know why she felt that way, because the bracelet on her arm wasn't warm or glowing. Then she realized the tree was deserted and her ears couldn't hear a single sound.

That is until she heard a soft beating noise behind her and turned. It was Queen Natta. "Everyone is out getting food," the ant told her.

"Where are my friends?" Litney asked.

"Up in my chambers, feasting."

After a moment, Litney cried, "Feasting? Oh no! Dokken—"

"Don't worry, Litney. Dokken isn't eating, although he wants to. Asta is just the opposite. She doesn't want to eat, but she knows she has to so she can be strong for you."

"Did she tell you about her son?'

"Yes."

"I feel as if it was my fault." Litney looked at her shoes.

Queen Natta led Litney over to a non-glowing mushroom and sat her down. "Anyone would, but that doesn't make it so. Now you have to focus on Mala. What is your plan?"

"I don't have one, that's the problem. Dokken and I thought we would just wander around until Mala found us, but every time that happens, I almost die."

"That's because Mala is in control," the queen told her.

"Exactly, so there's no hope."

"Sure there is," Queen Natta said.

"How?" Litney asked.

"There's hope if *you* are the one in control."

Litney shook her head. "That won't happen. That can't happen. How can I be in control? Mala is far more powerful than I am, than I could ever hope to be."

"Mala might be stronger than you are, but that doesn't mean you can't be in control. Have you ever ridden a horse?" Queen Natta asked.

"Yes."

"Is a horse bigger than you?"

Litney giggled and looked at her especially small current stature. "Yes."

"But when you rode the horse, could you get it to do what you wanted?"

A look passed over Litney's face. "I could—with the bit. It let me control the horse."

"Now of course the horse could have bolted or done all sorts of unpredictable things, but, yes, if everything went well, you could for that moment control something far more powerful than yourself."

Excited now, Litney asked, "But how would that work with Mala? I never know what form she'll take so I don't know what I could use."

Queen Natta looked at Litney's wrist.

"The bracelet?" Litney asked. "But so far, the bracelet has done everything. I don't really know how to use it."

"Maybe that should change."

"How?"

Queen Natta said, "What did the young hummingbird tell you?"

"That the person who wore the bracelet can fly," Litney recalled with a flutter in her stomach.

"And can you?"

"I . . . I don't know. I haven't tried."

Queen Natta swept her two right arms around the empty space they found themselves in. "There's plenty of room, and no one's watching." The ant smiled and tapped the ground with her foot. "Plus, the ground is soft."

Ever since she could remember, Litney had wanted nothing more than to be able to fly. She used to sit on the windowseat in her bedroom and stare at the sky, watching the birds, how they could catch updrafts and almost disappear from sight because they had flown so high. And she loved the

119

hawks drawing huge circles on the blue paper of sky. What freedom. What joy to be up where there was no noise or people—just air and wind and sky.

But now that flying was more than a daydream, she had no idea how to go about trying. Embarrassed because Queen Natta was watching, she jumped a few inches into the air only to come back down as predictably as she always had. Half-heartedly, she tried several more times, finally shrugging. "I guess I can't."

Queen Natta said, "You don't want to."

"What? Of course I want to," Litney protested. "I've always wanted to fly."

"Doesn't look like it to me."

Litney stamped her foot. "Because I feel silly—I know how stupid I must look."

"You look stupid because you aren't trying. When a person is trying, she never looks stupid," Queen Natta said.

"But if I try and I fail . . ." Litney didn't finish her sentence because she was afraid she might start to cry.

"If you try," the queen said, "then you've tried. It doesn't matter what the result is."

Still embarrassed, Litney turned her back on the Queen. She was right, of course. Her gaze went to the bracelet on her wrist. It felt comfortably warm, waiting. "I have always wanted to fly," she whispered to the beautiful piece of jewelry. "I have wanted to feel sky instead of ground. I know I can't do it on my own, but if you can help me, I will try with every bit of my being." Litney heard the queen behind her gasp. "What?" Litney asked. "What's wrong?"

"Look at your feet," the queen said.

Litney's feet hovered several inches off the ground. "Oh, my," she whispered. "I'm . . . I'm floating."

The queen clapped her hands together—all four of them. "Now, try flying," she said.

Litney tipped her head up and lifted the arm with the bracelet toward the ceiling of the tree. At first she didn't think anything was happening, but then she noticed the ceiling was getting closer and closer. When she looked down at Queen Natta, she didn't even try and hide her joy. "I'm flying!" she shouted. "I'm flying!"

"Yes!" the Queen yelled back. "But watch where you're going!"

The rough ceiling of the tree was approaching quickly, and Litney wasn't sure how to stop herself from crashing into it. Feeling a bit like Superman, she lowered her wrist until her arm stuck straight out in front of her. Now instead of flying up, she began to fly forward, her feet trailing behind her. Around and around, up and down she flew, crashing into the wall only once when she didn't get herself turned around in time.

Pointing her fist toward the ground, she slowly lowered until her feet returned to earth once again. "I flew."

The Queen had never seen a smile so big. "You sure did."

"I wonder what else I can do," Litney said. "What do some of the stories say?"

"What stories?" Dokken asked from the other side of the tree.

"Dokken!" Litney said, running over to him. "It's true—I can fly."

"Really? Oh, man, I've always wanted to fly. You sure I can't try the bracelet on for just one minute?'

Dokken had been through so much, done so much for her that Litney was tempted, but all she said was, "No, better not."

"I'm flattered that you wanted to," Dokken said.

"Hey, that's the second time you have done that."

"Done what?" Dokken asked.

"Read my mind," Litney answered.

"But I don't have the bracelet or anything—it must have just been coincidence, right?" Dokken looked to Queen Natta for an answer.

"I don't know. It could be you have received powers somehow as well as you moved from your world into this one."

"That's right," Litney said. "The Rock That Boils told me creatures that moved from one world to another sometimes gained powers."

"Why don't you see if it's really true?" the queen asked.

"Okay, think of something," Dokken ordered Litney. Then he smiled. "No, I didn't eat anything with the others."

"Good," she said.

"Try again," Dokken told her. After a moment, he said, "I'm scared, too."

"That's right," Litney said.

Dokken smiled. "Hey, I kinda like this. My father's always saying to my mother, 'Honey, I can't read your mind.' It always sounds like he would be a lot happier if he could."

Litney narrowed her eyes and crossed her arms over her chest. "This could be useful, but I don't want you knowing everything I think."

Dokken said, "Yeah, that would be too weird for words. I can only do it when I really concentrate. Like right now I'm not thinking about it, and so I can't tell what you're thinking."

"Okay, but let's keep it that way. Deal?" Litney put out her hand.

"Deal," Dokken replied, shaking it.

Litney sniffed. "Do you smell something?"

Dokken raised his nose to the air. "Maybe smoke?"

"That's what I smell."

Queen Natta's face grew serious and her wings began to thrum. Hovering, she said, "If there's a fire somewhere nearby, we need to see how big it is."

"I'll come with you," Litney said, pointing her bracelet up. Before she flew away with the Queen, she called back to Dokken over her shoulder, "Get Sensho and Asta. If you have to get out of here, we'll all meet at the hill where we sat for the Song of Silence."

"You really can fly!" Dokken shouted as he ran to find the others.

AS SHE AND THE QUEEN FLEW out of the tree, Litney wondered if she would return to full-size. She hoped not and so was pleased when they got outside and she hadn't changed. "The smell is getting stronger," Litney said to the Queen.

"Yes, there, can you see?"

Under the spread of the trees, Litney saw a small orange glow that seemed to be spreading quickly. Very quickly.

When they got closer to where the fire was, the Queen said, "I have to warn the forest. The sooner we can do that, the more lives we can save. You see if you can figure out how the fire started."

"Good luck," Litney said, unable to shake the feeling that she and the Queen would not see one another again. "And thank you."

"I fear you won't have any more time to work with the bracelet," the Queen answered, obviously torn between warning all of the animals and wanting to say goodbye.

Litney worried about this as well, but said, "I don't have much choice—I'll learn what I can as I go."

"Good luck to you. Be safe and strong." She gave Litney a hug.

"I will," Litney said and waved as she headed toward the small clouds of smoke that were just beginning to rise above the trees. She stopped at one of the edges of the fire and could soon see that the fire was spreading in the direction of the Hiding Tree. But where did it start? And how?

She was following the edge around to the other side when something on the ground caught her eye.

"What is that?" Litney asked, lowering herself into a nearby tree to get a closer look. Later, it would occur to her that she had grown to the size of a squirrel and managed the branches as nimbly as one of those creatures might, but now, her only thought was to get closer. She climbed down until she was finally close enough to see that there were actually two creatures standing in a small meadow. These odd creatures looked like puddles of silver standing up. Once again, their eyes were the same glowing green that Litney had seen in Mala's eyes. Litney stifled a gasp—one of the puddles had just grown an arm that shot fire. When the other creature grew an arm, it was obvious from the reaction of the wild and sucking flames that wind came from it. If Litney didn't do something to stop them, this fire would soon consume the whole forest and everything in it.

Litney knew that wishing she had more time to figure out how to use the bracelet wasn't going to help her now. Water, she needed water. She looked at the forest floor for any source of water, big or small. There was none. She scanned the sky, but it was a complete blue except for the clouds of smoke. Without knowing if it would do any good, Litney pointed the bracelet at the almost nonexistent clouds. "Grow, grow big and angry," she whispered over and over. "Big and angry. Big and angry."

At first, Litney couldn't tell if the clouds were growing because of what she was doing or simply because the fire was also growing. Soon, however, the blue sky was gone, covered instead by clouds that were heavy and full.

Concentrating, Litney changed her chant to one that sounded a lot like the one she had learned growing up. "Rain, rain, come today. Rain, rain, don't stay away. Rain, rain, come today. Rain, rain, please don't stay away."

Then she heard raindrops slapping the clumps of needles around her. She didn't allow herself to feel any relief—not yet. The fire was still growing and fast. "Heavier, heavier. Please, it has to be heavier."

Thunder rumbled across the sky, and the two silver creatures looked up. Litney could tell by the way they stood that they were angry. Each creature raised both hands and flames blasted out.

"Heavier, heavier," Litney chanted, praying she would win this battle between her and the creatures. She had to save the forest; she had to win.

Rain gushed from the sky now in dense sheets, the sound thunderous against the branches and trunks of the pines. Litney saw one of the silver creatures quit trying to make the flames grow. Instead, it looked around, and Litney knew it was trying to find her. She scampered around to the back side of the tree trunk and peeked out. The creature had spotted her. It didn't run—it flowed to her tree and began rolling up the trunk toward her. Litney lifted out an arm and flew up into the rain, the huge drops nearly blinding her. She worried that the creature could fly, that it was following her, but after several minutes of flying, she was convinced that she was alone.

She had escaped.

∗ 13 ∗

Gone

*T*HE FIRE WAS OUT; THE FOREST and the Hiding Tree were saved. When Litney landed beside Asta and Sensho at the hill by the Field of Fire, she saw a crowd of animals had gathered. They started to applaud.

"It wasn't me," Litney said, blushing. "It was the bracelet." When she held up her wrist, the animals grew silent and bowed. "But—" Litney began to protest.

"Hush," Asta whispered. "Just bow back."

Litney's body was stiff from uncertainty as she bowed to all of the animals. Straightening herself up again, she vowed, "I will do what I can to protect you, to protect all of us from Mala."

"We will help you in any way you need," a little striped chipmunk said.

"Yes. Yes," the animals murmured, their tone full of respect and conviction.

"I thank you." Litney bowed again, still feeling awkward but not knowing what else to do. "It should be safe for you to return to your homes. I'll call you when I need you."

Litney waited for the animals to leave before she asked, "Where's Dokken? I want all of us to sit down and plan. Queen Natta said that if I can be in control—" Litney stopped. "What?" she asked Sensho. "What's wrong?"

"Dokken's gone," the skunk replied.

"Where did he go?"

"We don't know," Asta said.

"What do you mean, you don't know?" Litney asked, her voice beginning to sound alarmed.

"When we were rushing around to warn all the animals, Dokken was with us," Sensho said.

"And then he was gone," Asta finished.

"Maybe he just got lost," Litney said, feeling somehow that wasn't what had happened.

"When all of the animals were gathered here, a deer said she saw Dokken being carried off by some creature she'd never seen before," Sensho said.

"What did the creature look like?" Litney asked, already knowing the answer.

"The deer said it was something silver with greenish glowing eyes."

Litney asked Asta, "Did the deer say when this happened?"

"Right at the end of the rain storm."

Instead of chasing her when she had flown away, Litney guessed that the creature had crawled back down the tree and found Dokken, taking him.

"What do we do?" Sensho asked.

"I was going to say that Queen Natta had said we needed to figure out how to get some control, and then find Mala, but now . . ." Litney felt lost. Dokken had been with her on this whole adventure. The two of them together had always figured out what to do. Litney looked at Sensho and Asta with tears in her eyes, "Just when I think I can do something . . ."

"We have to do something," Sensho said. "Dokken's been taken. We have to find him."

"Yes," Litney agreed. "The first thing we need to do is get Dokken back."

"Possibly," Asta said, "but there's also a bigger picture we need to be concerned with. It's obvious that Dokken was taken to stop you and the bracelet. Mala must know how close the two of you are. Right now the only way she can get you is by getting to you, which is why she took Dokken."

Litney's entire body showed her rage and frustration. She narrowed her eyes and clenched her fists. Suddenly she lifted one wrist and shot up into the air.

"Litney! What are you doing? Where are you going?" Asta called.

"I'm finding Dokken."

"But wait, we need a plan," Asta called.

"No! I'm going to take care of Mala once and for all."

"Litney!" Asta called again, but the sky was empty and the girl was gone.

LITNEY WASN'T SURE WHERE SHE WAS GOING, but she knew she couldn't just sit around doing nothing while Mala had Dokken. She had to get him back.

Not knowing what else to do, she returned to the small meadow where she had last seen the silver creatures who had started the fire. When she arrived, she saw smoke rising from the charred grass. She surveyed the damage—the fire had affected an area about the size of two football fields, but the tall pines at the edges had suffered little. The grass fire had run along the ground under them, burning too quickly to start their trunks afire. Litney was surprised but thankful there hadn't been more damage. No creatures—with glowing green eyes or otherwise—were anywhere to be seen.

"Mala!" Litney shouted. "Mala, I know you have Dokken." She flew back and forth over the field. "Mala! Mala!"

Something smashed into Litney from behind, and her body went tumbling downward. She managed to right herself just before she crashed into the ground, and her feet ran along the burnt-up grass. She returned to the air, only to be knocked to the ground again. This time her body hit the black field hard, and the wind got knocked out of her. Before she could move, a screaming filled her ears, and she felt claws digging into her arm. Luckily it was the wrong arm because the wrist with the bracelet was tucked safely under her body. With every last bit of strength she had, Litney rolled over and hit her attacker with the bracelet. There was another scream, and she was free. Litney scrambled to her feet and ran to hide behind a tree.

Her attacker, who had landed, stood before her. Litney assumed it was Mala, but the thing that stood in front of her looked like nothing she had ever seen before. The creature was tall, as tall as two of Litney's fathers standing one on top of the other. And it was purple—a purple that shifted between bright wisteria flowers and cloudy like the sky. Her mother would have known the word to use to describe it: mottled. The creature had no feathers or hair. Its skin was smooth and shiny, as if it had just stepped out of water, and its eyes glowed green. On one side of its head, a thin stream of dark purple trickled down. That might have been where the bracelet had hit. Litney hoped so. That would be some small proof that this creature was not invincible.

"Mala?" Litney asked.

"Yes," Mala answered, and this time, her voice was shrill and scraping.

Relieved that, for the moment, Mala wasn't coming any nearer, Litney worked up her courage to ask, "How did you get the bracelet to come early?"

"Why should I tell you, stupid one?" Mala taunted.

Litney bristled, but answered, "If I'm so stupid, the only way I'm going to know how you are powerful enough to be doing this is if you tell me."

"Nice try. But that doesn't really give me a reason why I should tell you."

Litney tried not to shudder at the sound of Mala's voice. It was like fingernails scraping down a blackboard. She said, "You want to tell me."

"I do, do I?" the creature asked.

"Yes."

"And why is that?"

Litney replied from her hiding spot behind the tree, "Because it's no fun to be powerful unless you tell others how you did it."

Mala laughed and answered, "You have no idea how much fun it can be to destroy things without saying anything at all."

Litney shivered, but pressed on. "You told Asta why you killed her son."

"What?" Mala asked.

"The bear cub that you killed after you couldn't kill me in the river. You told Asta why you'd done it. Why would you do that unless you

130

felt the need to gloat? You want to tell me how you were powerful enough to get the bracelet to appear early so you could move freely into any world you wanted."

"Hmmm," Mala said. "Maybe you aren't as stupid as I thought. All right then, I will tell you. As I'm sure you've been told, finding a key from one world into the next is easy enough. A little bribe here, a little pain there. You'd be amazed how quickly creatures are willing to give up important things."

"If it's so easy, why do you need the bracelet?" Litney asked.

"It might be easy to get the keys, but it takes time. Time to find them, time to find ways to get them. I want a key that lets me into any world any time I want." The evil smile on Mala's face made Litney tremble. The creature continued, "I happened to be in a world three worlds away from this one, and I discovered a book. Most of the book was useless. It told of the small keys and how to get them. But the final chapter was on the three keys that can move you anywhere you want."

"Three?" Litney asked. "I thought there were only two."

"One has never been seen, and there are only rumors about its existence. I didn't look for that one. The other key has not been seen in five hundred years. The last time it was seen was during the time of a great flood in the world it was in. Many fear it's been lost forever. That leaves the bracelet." Mala pointed at Litney's wrist.

"Still, that doesn't explain how you were powerful enough to make the bracelet appear two years early."

"You know all those pretty faces that appeared to you at the Song of Silence?"

"H-how could you know about that?" Litney stammered.

Mala sneered. "Did you forget we were discussing how powerful I am? I found my way to the world that the bracelet comes from—I watched everything they do. They are a peaceful people with no weapons and no power. Except for the bracelet. Knowing that it wasn't time yet for the bracelet to come to you, I told them to give it to me. To show them I was serious, many of them had to die. Finally, they said they couldn't give me the bracelet because they had already sent it to you." A look of fury passed over Mala's face at their act of defiance, but then Mala smiled, once again under control. "Not that it mattered. I have great power in this world as well, so it'll be easy for me to take it from you, a stupid, worthless girl. Now, here I am, finally looking at the bracelet. I will have it. Give it to me."

"Wait a minute!" Litney said, alarmed when Mala began to move closer.

Mala said. "I'm not going to ask again. Give me the bracelet."

"No," Litney said.

"I thought you'd say that, you stubborn and stupid child."

"Stop calling me stupid! I'm not stupid!"

Mala screamed so loudly that Litney had to cover her ears, and still the piercing in her eardrums was almost unbearable. Suddenly, all was silent, and Litney looked up. The silver creatures who had started the fire had appeared and they were holding Dokken between them.

"Dokken!" Litney shouted, wanting to leave the meager protection the tree provided her to go to him, but knowing she had better not.

Dokken didn't answer. He hung limply from the hands that held him.

Hoping he had enough energy to read her mind, Litney thought, *Dokken, I'm here. Dokken, are you okay? Look up if you can. Let me know you can hear me.* Litney waited and didn't breathe. Finally Dokken looked up for the briefest moment before his head fell forward once again.

"Doesn't look so good, does he?" Mala asked as she ran a long purple finger around his face.

"Get your hands off him," Litney threatened.

"Or what? You'll hurt me?"

Litney hated that sneer, but she needed to focus to help Dokken. "What have you done to him?"

"What is it that you humans say? Oh—that's for me to know and you to find out."

"It's me you want, Mala. Let him go."

"Now we're getting somewhere. I'll be happy to let him go. All you have to do is give me the bracelet. Simple enough, wouldn't you agree?"

Litney considered it for a moment, but then she heard a voice in her head shout *NO!* It was Dokken. Somehow, she could hear Dokken's voice in her head. She heard the voice again, weaker this time, *Litney, no matter what, don't do it.*

"Give me the bracelet," Mala repeated.

Litney wanted to rush to Dokken, but she knew she couldn't. She knew she had to keep the bracelet safe and away from Mala. She swallowed the tears that had begun to sting her eyes and stood taller. "No."

Mala screamed and then stalked back to where Dokken was. "Oh, how I want to kill you!" she screamed in the boy's ear. He jumped in shock and pain, but then he raised his eyes and stared at her.

"Fine," he whispered. "Go ahead. Do it." In his head, he told Litney, *Now, run. Go.*

I can't leave you.

You have to.

Mala lifted a hand to Dokken's throat and began to squeeze, but then it appeared she changed her mind. "No. I'm going to give you something worse than death." Mala made a whistling sound and the silver things dropped Dokken to the ground. Then they clapped their hands together

133

and from their hands, Litney could see food beginning to form. There was a turkey leg, an ice cream cone, a bowl of popcorn. "Hungry?" Mala asked Dokken.

In her mind, Litney shouted, *Dokken get up. Run. I'll save you. I promise.* Dokken did nothing. Was he under some sort of spell? He must be.

"Well, I think you're hungry. Here, have some food." While the two silver creatures held him immobile, Mala shoved the ice cream cone into Dokken's mouth. He struggled a little, but not enough to escape Mala's hand, which was working his mouth up and down, up and down. Then Litney saw it—she saw Dokken's throat contract.

"No!" Litney yelled, but it was too late.

He had swallowed. Dokken lifted his head up and Mala gave him some more ice cream.

"Dokken, stop!" Litney shouted, but she knew it didn't matter. Trembla had said if they tasted even a crumb, they would know a hunger like they had never known before. Somehow Mala must have known this.

It wasn't long before Dokken was standing of his own volition, before he was shoveling food into his mouth. The silver creatures produced more and more food, and Dokken shoved it all into his mouth, grunting.

Mala laughed. "Fill up, little piggy. Eat while you can."

"Mala, stop it!" Litney cried, tears streaming down her face.

"You're right," Mala said, clapping her hands together. "Food, be gone." And it was.

Dokken fell to his knees and began to whimper, sniffing the ground. He crawled over to the silver creatures and begged, "Please, please. Food. Give me food. I'll do anything."

Mala's underlings brushed him off, but Mala walked over to him. "Dokken," she said in a saccharin voice.

Dokken was panting, and his eyes were glazed. He seemed possessed.

"Dokken," Mala repeated, shaking him slightly.

His eyes focused.

"Do you want food?" Mala asked as if she were a mother asking her child if he wanted to eat.

Dokken grunted, and Litney covered her mouth with her hand to keep her from sobbing out loud.

"She has food," Mala said, pointing at Litney. "Go and get it."

With sounds of pig, dog, and other unnameable animals, Dokken lunged at Litney. She raised her wrist and flew up into the air, narrowly avoiding his grabbing hands.

"Not so fast," Mala said, hurtling toward her.

"I wish I could disappear," Litney said and knew she must have when Mala flew right past her.

Mala screamed in frustration. "Where is she?" she asked the creatures, who shrugged since the girl was nowhere to be seen.

"Is this how you want to play?" Mala asked, alighting on the ground once again. "Fine. Let's see how you like this." Mala grabbed Dokken and began twisting his arm. The boy, ravenously starving as he was, still screamed out in pain.

Litney reappeared. "Stop!" She shouted. "I'm right here."

"Land!" Mala commanded.

Litney complied, and when her feet touched the ground, Dokken charged her once again.

"Protect me," Litney whispered, praying the bracelet would do something. When Dokken's fingers were about six inches from her face, they bounced backward. This frustrated Dokken even more, and he began to scrape and scratch and claw at the air, but he couldn't reach her.

"Do you want me to hurt him?" Mala asked.

"No," Litney whispered, trying to remember this was not the Dokken that she knew. He would have never hurt her. It was fierce magic that was making him act this way.

"Then give me the bracelet."

"No," Litney whispered again. "I'm sorry Dokken. I'll save you if I can, but for now, I have to go. Goodbye." Litney disappeared.

And heard Mala scream.

* 14 *

Planning and Preparation

OU MADE MALA BLEED?" Sensho asked Litney. The two of them were sitting in a circle with close to a dozen other birds, insects, and animals planning what could be done to destroy Mala. They were on the dirt floor of a rabbit warren—some animals had needed the bracelet's help to shrink enough to fit inside.

"I don't know if she bleeds like you and I do," Litney said, "but I definitely hurt her."

"How?" a dragonfly asked. He had been forced to join the circle late because he couldn't remember the password. The rabbits posted outside all of the holes were very serious about their jobs as sentries.

"With the bracelet. She was on top of me, and I hit her with the bracelet. Later I noticed a wound where the bracelet had made contact."

"But you aren't sure it was a wound or that it was caused by the bracelet?" Asta clarified.

Litney poked at the dirt by her feet. "No."

"And so all of this could really mean nothing. We could go in there with a plan, and it could be that you can't hurt Mala at all," Asta said.

Litney poked harder at the dirt. "Yes."

Asta took a paw and gently lifted the girl's chin. "I do not want to see you get hurt, that's all."

"I know, I know. It's just, I really believe I hurt her. In my heart."

"Then it must be true," Sensho said excitedly.

"Why?" a frog asked.

"Because of the Song of Silence. Didn't the faces tell you to trust your heart?"

"Yes," Litney said, brightening for the first time in a while. It was all she could do to get her mind off Dokken. His face. His eyes. "Yes, they did."

"And you believe, in your heart, that you hurt Mala?" Asta persisted. At some point she had gone from having to protect this girl to wanting to protect her.

"Yes." This time, Litney's voice was strong and sure.

"Then let's make this plan."

THEY TALKED THROUGH MOST of the night. Toward daybreak, a tired but satisfied Asta asked, "Is everyone clear on what they're supposed to do?"

All the creatures nodded, except for Lando, another bear. He shrugged his big shoulders. "Yeah, I guess."

"What's wrong?" Asta asked a little sharply but only because it had been such a long night.

"I don't know," Lando sighed. "It just doesn't seem like it'll work. Mala's very, very powerful."

Litney could have sworn she saw the bear shudder.

"We know that, but I think our plan plays to our strengths and Mala's weaknesses," Sensho said. The other animals nodded their agreement.

"Maybe, but what if Mala . . ." Lando began.

"What if Mala what?" Asta asked.

"What if Mala were to attack us before—" Lando never finished his thought. Instead he lunged at Litney, clawing at her right shoulder and down her arm, the arm with the bracelet on it.

Litney screamed and tried to scramble backwards, but she pressed up against the dirt wall behind her back.

"What are you doing?" Asta yelled, throwing her powerful arms around the other bear before he could hurt Litney any more.

Lando tried to shake Asta off. "I've got to kill her. Kill her!"

Litney tried to point the bracelet at Lando, hoping it would do something to save her, but she couldn't move her right arm. It hung there at her side, bleeding heavily.

Asta slammed Lando against a wall, and she and Sensho and all the other creatures formed a barrier between Lando and Litney. "What are you doing? Are you crazy?" Asta demanded. She had known Lando since they had both been cubs. He had always been a good, kind-hearted bear.

Lando glanced at Asta, but he seemed most concerned with the backside of the porcupine and Sensho's tail, both of which were pointed right at his nose. "Let me at her," he growled.

"No," Sensho said.

"I have to kill her," Lando pleaded.

"Why?" Asta asked.

"Because," Lando said. "Because if I don't, Mala will—will kill my family."

"She'll what?" Sensho asked.

Lando trembled with indecision, then sat down, defeated. "Yesterday, we met another group of bears. They said they had gotten lost. Wanted us to help them find some food. It seemed odd, but the little cubs looked like they were starving. Thin. Not round like a cub is supposed to be this time of year. So we led them to a patch of berries. I went in front to lead the way. When I looked back, I saw that they had my family in huge nets. That's when I saw one had changed into something purple and huge."

"Mala," Litney whispered.

Lando nodded. "Mala told me she'd kill them all if I didn't kill her." Lando thrust his nose at Litney, who was looking paler and paler. "I had no choice. I'm sorry. I'm so sorry." The bear began to sob.

"Lando, it wasn't right," Asta said, then added quietly, "but we understand." She put a paw out to Lando. "We'll do what we can to get your family back to you, safe and sound."

Lando looked at Asta's paw and put his own on it.

Now that the danger had passed, Sensho quickly turned his attention to Litney. It didn't take more than a glance to know that the girl was in serious trouble. "She's lost a lot of blood."

The dragonfly said, "We have to get her to the Hive."

SHE LOOKED AT HER ARM—OH, HOW RED IT WAS. It looked like rose petals were all over her arm, or apple peels. The red was moving—more and more tumbled down her arm. It was so odd—she would hear a *thud* and then a little more red would come. *Thud.* Red. *Thud.* Red.

140

Her head was a little whirly. It wasn't a bad feeling; she just felt all warm and floaty. Not like she had felt when she was flying—then she had felt strong and quick. Now she felt light, as if there was nothing to keep her from floating up and away forever.

Now, instead of the *thud thud* she heard something else. A hum. And voices. She couldn't understand what the voices were saying. *Hmmmmmmmmmm*, she tried to say in return, smiling. Her body vibrated. *Hmmmmmmm*.

Something warm was crawling up her body. It started at her toes, now it was at her ankles, her knees, up up. Oh, it was lovely. Warm and smooth. It stopped when it reached her neck. She felt someone take her head and gently tip it backwards. It came to rest on something soft and spongy.

Hmmmmmm she said again, hoping someone would know she was trying to say thank you.

Litney tried to open her eyes to put form to the voices in her head.

". . . do you think . . . how long . . . make it?"

". . . hard . . . time . . . let's see."

But she couldn't.

Litney opened her eyes and looked around her. It was so golden and smelled so sweet that she thought she must be in heaven.

She just hadn't expected heaven to be so thick.

"Litney," someone said. "Come on, Litney. It's time to get up."

Litney rolled her head to one side and then the other. She had been having a dream.

About a boy.

A dog.

A turtle.

There was a house.

"Litney," the voice said more strongly. "It's time for you to wake up. We need you."

Litney tried to wake up, but her eyes, her head, her everything felt heavy. "Can't," she mumbled.

"But you must. Remember Dokken. Remember all of the creatures counting on you. Remember the bracelet."

Litney's arm began to grow warm. And itchy. What effort it took to reach her other arm across her body to scratch it.

"Good, Litney," the voice said. "The more you can move, the quicker you'll wake up."

Litney scratched and scratched at her arm, but instead of finding relief, the itching had only begun. The bracelet's warmth began to flow up her arm and branch out all over her body. She had to scratch her neck, her chin, her stomach. This was difficult because her skin was sticky, and her fingers kept getting stuck to her body. "I'm . . . so . . . itchy!" Litney panted.

"That's because you've been lying in a pool of honey for the past three days. We just got done draining it, and so your circulation is coming back to normal."

With the blood flowing freely through her body once again, Litney's mind began to clear. The boy, the dog—it hadn't been just a dream. "Dokken!" she said, struggling to stand but falling back to her seat. "You said I was in honey for three days. That means he's been with Mala for three days. What if, what if . . ." she couldn't bring herself to finish the thought.

"He's fine," the voice said.

For the first time, Litney turned her head to see who was speaking. It was the dragonfly that had been in the rabbit warren. His wings, a cross between prisms and stained-glass windowpanes, caught the soft golden light, breaking it into a million pieces.

"I'm sorry," Litney said, "but I have forgotten your name."

"Heak."

"How do you know?' Litney asked.

"I know my own name," the dragonfly said, worried that the girl had lost too much blood.

"No, I mean how do you know that Dokken's okay?"

Relieved, Heak answered, "We have our ways."

"How?" Litney persisted. She had to know that Dokken was okay.

"Spies," the dragonfly whispered, checking over his shoulder. He needn't have worried—the hive was empty.

"Spies? But what if Mala discovers them? Won't they be in danger?" Litney asked. So many people had already been hurt by all of this.

"Spies know that there's always a danger. But I doubt that Mala will notice *our* spies."

Litney was not convinced. "Why?"

"Because they're dandelion seeds. They watch her and when they have something to report, they simply let go and sail to one of us," Heak explained.

Litney was impressed. She could also tell the dragonfly was growing impatient. "I'm sorry. I just wouldn't be able to handle it if something had happened to Dokken."

"Your concern is admirable," the dragonfly said, "but you also have bigger things to worry about."

"Mala," Litney said.

"Yes, but even before that, we have to get your strength back."

Litney remembered what Lando had done to her arm. She looked down and saw bright red rows trailing from her shoulder to her wrist. The wounds were closed, but barely. "How?"

"We'll take you to another bath," Heak said.

"Will it get rid of some of this stickiness?" Litney asked. When she lifted her elbow from her side, long stringy strands of honey formed.

"Yes, but more importantly, it will help your wounds."

"Is it here in the hive?" Litney wanted to know.

"No, we need to fly to get there." When Litney started to raise her arm to fly, Heak stopped her. "Why don't you get on my back? That way your arm can rest a little longer."

"Okay." Litney was relieved—dizzying pain had darted up to her shoulder when she had tried lifting her arm. Her shoulder throbbed some, but when it was down by her side, it was at least bearable.

Litney climbed on the dragonfly's back. They sped out of the hole. As they flew through the forest, Litney asked, "How are Asta and Sensho?"

"Fine. They've been busy making sure everything's ready for when we need them."

"What's Mala been up to since I've been in the hive?" Litney asked.

Heak was pleased Litney had asked that. It showed she hadn't lost her focus or resolve. "She's been surprisingly quiet."

"Did she hurt Lando's family?" Litney asked.

"No. The dandelion seeds told us Dokken and Lando's family are all being held in two caves, one right next to the other," Heak answered.

"Do we know where?"

"Yes."

"Well, then we have to go and save them," Litney said, trying to raise her right arm and ignore the pain so she could fly. "We can't let Mala hurt them."

Heak was glad when the girl dropped her hand with a *huff,* unable to fly. "As I said, little one, your concern is admirable, but we must remember this is bigger than one boy, one family."

Litney bristled at the dragonfly's words. "How heartless! What if it was your family that Mala held hostage? How would you feel then?"

"I'd do everything in my power to make sure Mala could never do it to anyone else's family. I'd do whatever was necessary to stop Mala and pray my family would come out of it all right," Heak said. "Litney, none of us wants to see anyone get hurt. But we need to remember how many could get hurt, how badly this could turn out if we don't keep our attention on Mala."

"That's true," Litney admitted. "But we also need to think about the very ones we're trying to save."

"You're right. And I believe our plan has done that. Don't you agree?"

It took Litney a moment to remember the details of the plan. "Yes."

"Good. Then let us stick to it," Heak said.

Litney laughed weakly. "I feel like I could stick to anything right now."

IN A FIELD OF DANDELIONS not far from the hive, Heak began to descend toward a pool about the size of a bathtub. It was lined with stones and filled with white liquid. To Litney it looked disgusting.

"What is that?" she asked.

"The milk of dandelions," Heak answered as he landed.

Litney slid off his back, not quickly or easily. "I have to soak in that?"

"Yes, it'll help you heal. And now I must leave," the dragonfly told her. "I have things to attend to, but I'll return soon."

"Okay," Litney said.

Heak could tell she was uncertain as to what she should do. "Why don't you get in the pool and then do as you're told."

"Thank you, Heak."

"You're welcome. Now get strong. For Dokken, for Lando's family. For all of us."

"I will." With her good arm, Litney waved to the dragonfly as he flew off. Since everything on her was already sticky from the honey, Litney decided she had to get into the pool of dandelion milk, clothes and all. "I hope there are no girl-eating fish in here," she said as she climbed into the liquid that felt as if it were exactly the same temperature as her body. Litney found a little shelf to sit on and she leaned her head back.

It wasn't long before she saw a ripple in the water in front of her. Something long and black surfaced. Alarmed, she clambered out of the pool, knocking her wounds against the stones as she did so. "Ouch!" she cried.

"Then you shouldn't have gotten out of the pool," a voice said.

Litney looked down into the water and saw the long black thing. It looked like a ribbon at least a foot long. It wasn't a snake—it was too flat. "What are you?" she asked.

"A leech."

"Eeew," Litney said before she could stop herself.

"Why 'eeew'?" the slippery creature wanted to know.

"I don't know. You suck blood, you look like a snake. You're just . . . eeew."

"We can be quite beautiful." To prove its point, the leech began what looked like a ballet of ribbon and water. It circled, fluttered, twisted and turned.

Litney had to admit it did look beautiful.

"And for three thousand years humans have been using us."

Litney remembered reading somewhere, probably one of her parents' books, about Napoleon's surgeon, who believed so much in the healing benefits of leeches that he had imported millions of them to France.

"What's your name?" Litney asked.

"I'm Longley," the leech answered.

"I'm Litney."

"It would be an honor to serve you, Litney, but if you'd rather not receive any help from me, that's fine. I simply want to do what I can to help the one with the bracelet."

When Longley put it that way, Litney felt badly that she had acted so squeamish. Still, the thought of letting a leech attach itself to her was almost more than she could bear. Trying to get out of this gracefully, she asked, "Thank you for wanting to help, but haven't I already bled enough?"

"From what Heak told me, you did lose a lot of blood. But how easy is it for you to raise your arm?" Longley asked. Litney tried, then shook her head. "My bite's designed to increase blood flow to damaged areas in a safe way. If I can do that with your wounds, it'll help you heal faster."

The leech didn't comment on how long it took Litney to get back into the water. In fact, once she had gotten settled, he offered, "Why don't you close your eyes? That might help relax you some."

Litney knew it was rude, but she couldn't stop a shudder as her eyes squeezed shut. "Is this going to hurt?"

"I don't think so, but let me know if it does."

"Okay," Litney said, every muscle in her body ready to bolt if anything gross touched her. Or if she felt the leech "strike," its mouth tearing at her flesh. She was about to open her eyes and ask what was taking so long when she felt the weirdest sensation on her right arm. At the farm, she often fed apples to her grandparents' horses, and their great lips would work the skin of her hand to pull off every last bit of the sweet fruit. That's what it felt like, as if lips were gently massaging her skin. The sensation was far from painful, but it was insistent. Soon, her arm grew warm, and she felt the rest of her body begin to relax. Even the dull throbbing pain she had experienced since getting out of the honey bath began to ebb away.

"WHAT?" LITNEY ASKED SOME TIME LATER, opening her eyes.

"I said you needed to wake up," Longley said. "I'm done."

"How long have I been asleep?"

"A couple of hours."

"Wow. It felt like you just started." Litney stretched her neck and climbed out of the pool. The redness of the wounds streaking down her arm had lessened, and when she moved and flexed her arm, she exclaimed, "It doesn't hurt!"

"Good," Longley said.

"And I can move it again."

"Good," Longley repeated.

Litney knelt down beside the pool and said, "I'm sorry."

"Some creatures are known for being beautiful. Some are known for their song. Some are known for creating fear. It is the way it is."

"I can't believe I'm saying this, but you're now in the category of creatures known for being beautiful."

The leech circled, then lowered his head. "Thank you. It was an honor to help you."

Litney looked around. "What do I do now?"

Longley said, "Someone will be coming for you soon. Wait here and enjoy the sunshine. It might be the last quiet you have for a while."

DOKKEN SQUEEZED HIS EYES SHUT, wishing he was somewhere else. Anywhere else. He even wished he was back in school, eating his bologna and mayonnaise sandwich, the same bologna and mayonnaise sandwich he told his mom he hated every single morning as she was making it. The rubbery pinkish gray of the bologna was simply, as Dokken was so fond of saying, too weird for words. That's why every single day, he peeled off the offending quiver of meat and wrapped it in his napkin as quickly as he could, making sure his skin never even touched it. But, boy, he'd eat that bologna right now, truckloads of it in fact, if he could only get out of here.

Because here, Mala was angry. That was obvious. When Dokken dared to open his eyes, he saw her as she stalked around the cave she was holding him in. He did his best to stay unobtrusive in the corner. He did not want to draw any attention to himself, especially when he heard her mumbling. ". . . have to get it . . . I must . . . that girl . . . have to get it . . . that girl . . . she *will* give it to me . . . how . . . hurt her but can't get my hands on her . . . hurt her . . . kill her . . . hurt . . . kill." Mala turned and saw Dokken.

Since her legs were so long, it took her only one step to get to him. She hauled him up by the neck, like a mother dog will do with a puppy, and shook him. "You're going to help me get the bracelet." It was not a question or a request. It was a demand, a threat even, because a threat implied bad things, very bad things, would happen if he didn't comply.

Mala continued. "We'll put you in a field somewhere and get that girl to come save you. It'll look like you're there all by yourself, like you managed to escape. When that girl lands on the ground, I'll get the bracelet."

"H-h-how are you going to do that?" he squeaked.

"With this." Mala pulled out a knife, the same knife that had been in Litney's back pack, the one that had released Litney from Mala's hands in the river.

149

"How did you get that?"

"We found your backpacks at the Field. You must have left them behind. Look, here's yours. So cute and quaint, why you even have a walking stick. Like you were some sort of adventurer. Are you an adventurer? A big strong adventurer?" She threw him to the ground. "Here's what I think of your adventure. I think I'm going to kill that girl with her very own knife and get the bracelet."

"You can't kill her," Dokken cowered as Mala stood above him.

"Who's going to stop me?" Mala hissed, bringing her face close enough to Dokken's so he could feel her breath on his face. "You?" she laughed. "You think you're going to stop me? Puny, helpless kid."

He was not puny. He was not helpless. He was not going to be that kid cringing in the bathroom stall anymore. He was not going to be some pawn that would lead Litney to her death. He would not let Mala hurt her. He was going to do something. He was going to be strong and act. He was going to fight for himself. He was going to fight for Litney, for all of them.

The sand he had grabbed flew out of his hand and toward Mala's eyes. As soon as she screamed, Dokken scrambled to his feet and dashed toward the mouth of the cave. It was his bad luck that Mala, in her flailing pain, was dancing around and happened to stick one of her legs out just as he was about to make it past.

Dokken tripped and went sprawling into the sand with an *ooooff*. Still clutching at her eyes, Mala grabbed in the direction of Dokken's noise.

Her hand found his throat.

* 15 *

The Battle

A FEW MINUTES AFTER LITNEY CLIMBED out of the pool, Heak, the dragonfly, returned and asked if she was ready. She nodded and flexed her arm—the leech had made it feel stronger than it ever had. Litney, flying under her own power, followed Heak back to where Asta and Sensho were. They waved to her from the ground and when she landed, their reunion was jubilant, but brief. It was time to move.

As they had planned, Litney flew to a nearby lake and shrank down until she was small enough to sit on the back of a frog out in the middle of a bay covered by lily pads. From there she was able to see everything. Fish of all colors and lengths formed an invisible blockade beneath the water's surface. On top, hundreds of ducks and geese floated like feathered flotillas. Along the shore, otter, mink, and beaver squished nervously in the mud. Gophers, raccoons, and coyotes stood in a small field, and the forest hid all manner of bird, deer, moose, wolf, and bear. They didn't know what Mala would do, but this way Litney felt she had some amount of control of the situation. Plus five lines of defenses had to be more than enough to defeat the evil creature.

When everyone had taken their place, Litney called, "Ready?"

The animals clamored in response.

"I want to thank you all for your bravery." She raised her hand in the air, "May the bracelet protect us all!"

After another cheer died down, Litney looked at the bracelet and whispered, "I hope you're ready." The bracelet glowed a little, then went dark. Not sure what that meant but with all the strength she had, Litney yelled, "Mala! It's time." While her voice wasn't painfully loud, it didn't die down as it normally would have. Instead, it seemed to pulse over the earth, until Litney was certain Mala had to have heard it.

"Now we wait," Litney whispered.

The silence that followed was almost as deep as what Litney had experienced during the Song of Silence. Except where that one had been peaceful, this one felt sinister. When her eyes began to sting from looking so hard, when she began to doubt that Mala had even heard her, Litney thought she saw something along the horizon. A huge moving band darkened the sky.

"Here they come," Litney cried, but she wasn't sure what they were. Even as the creatures got nearer and nearer, it was nearly impossible to make out what they were. The closer they got, the more obvious it became that they weren't any normal kind of bird. For one thing, they were huge—each bird's wingspan was the length of three or four Litney's height. And they didn't have feathers. Instead, they were covered with what looked like black leather. Each bird wore a small helmet and when they got close enough, everyone could see their eyes glowed green.

"What are those?" the frog Litney was sitting on asked, agitated and shifting on the lily pad.

BETSY JOHNSON-MILLER

"I don't know," she answered. When she saw how unsettled the animals around her were getting, she yelled, "Be strong."

The flying things arrived more quickly than anyone thought possible and soon began divebombing the animals in the field and along the shore. The huge avians seemed to consume the space in front of Litney, and the smaller animals were no match for them. While some animals took to the water and while the coyotes did their best to fend off the storm of birds, it soon become obvious that something else had to be done. Asta decided it was time to command the animals hidden in the forest to come out and help.

At her command, the bigger animals flooded the field from their hiding places in the forest in an effort to fend off the birds. They were slightly more successful than the smaller animals, but the birds were so large and so many, it began to look hopeless.

And it got worse. A hundred or more of the silvery creatures like the ones that had started the forest fire descended from a cloud in the sky. With skill and precision they sawed through the trees at the edge of the forest. It would have taken a normal person with a chainsaw several minutes to topple any of those big pines. These creatures, however, with laser-like arms, managed to fell two trees (one with each arm) in under thirty seconds.

From her perch on the frog, Litney watched the silvery creatures, uncertain of why they were doing what they were doing. It took her several minutes to see that the fallen trees began to form a barricade, effectively cutting off any retreat to the forest. Litney knew all of their defenses now were either in the open field or in the water.

"Fly!" Sensho cried when he, too, realized what was happening. The birds in the water took to the air, hoping to slow the progress of the silver creatures. As they flew over the black birds in the field and reached

153

the edge of the forest, however, a horde of turquoise bugs the size of quarters burst out of the ground and swarmed around the birds. The birds couldn't see, and many of the beetle-like bugs flew into the birds' mouths so that they could no longer breathe either.

Litney saw nearly every animal and bird falling to the ground and not getting back up again. They were no match for the strength of Mala's forces. She recalled Asta's words: *No matter what's happening, you have to keep hidden. You and the bracelet must stay concealed at all costs. That's the only way we can make sure you remain safe.*

But Litney wasn't about to let the animals die to keep her safe.

"Mala!" Litney shouted, growing to her full size and flying up above the water. "Stop this! Here I am. Take me."

The fighting stopped abruptly, and after a moment of stunned silence, all the creatures Mala controlled lifted a raucous shriek of victory that made Litney's body shake. The beetles thronged around her, carrying her away from the water, the shore, the forest. *No!* Litney thought she heard someone shouting, but the wings of the beetles were so loud, she couldn't have been sure.

LITNEY SAT IN THE CAVE for what seemed like hours before Mala arrived. Several times she thought about escaping—she could make herself invisible and slip past the five silver creatures posted outside the mouth of the cave, or she could become a worm and crawl under them. But she knew it was time that she and Mala had this out once and for all.

"If you set Dokken and Lando's family free," Litney began as soon as the creature appeared.

Mala walked over to the girl and struck her across the face. "Silence!" the beast screamed. "You might have the bracelet, but I'm in charge. And to prove it . . ." Mala whistled. Two silvery creatures dragged in Dokken.

"Dokken?" Litney said. He didn't say anything.

"Your friend and I have gotten to know each other very well over the past few days, but where have you been? It just wasn't as much fun without you here."

"You know exactly where I was," Litney said through clenched teeth.

"Hmm, by the looks of your arm, you had a run-in with something large. A bear perhaps?"

"How is Lando's family?" Litney demanded.

"So concerned about everyone else. How noble," Mala said. "Perhaps you should be concerned with yourself. You seem to think that bracelet gives you enough power to defeat me. We both know that isn't going to happen."

"Yes, it will," Litney vowed.

"I don't think so."

"Why not?" Litney asked.

"Because what's so good and noble about you will also be your downfall."

"What are you talking about?"

Mala waved a purple hand, and the two creatures dropped Dokken. He didn't move.

Litney tried to rush forward, but Mala pushed her, sending the girl flying back onto the sandy floor of the cave. "Do you not have ears to hear?" Mala shouted. "I am in charge!" Mala's purple form stalked over to Dokken, grabbed him by the back of the neck and said, "Not that it matters. The boy's dead."

"Wh-what?" Litney whispered.

"DEAD!"

"But, but." Litney's chest began to rise and fall rapidly until it became almost impossible to breathe. "No," she whispered. "It can't be true."

Mala dropped Dokken onto the sand. "You don't believe me? Come see for yourself."

Litney crawled over to Dokken and shook him. "Dokken? Dokken?" The boy's skin was cold and sickeningly white beneath all his freckles. "No, noo, you didn't." As if that wasn't more than she could bear, while Litney wept over the boy's body, Mala snuck up behind her and tore the bracelet off her arm.

LITNEY SOBBED QUIETLY. SHE COULDN'T bring herself to look at Dokken lying at Mala's feet.

"Don't tell me you actually thought you were going to defeat me," Mala said with a laugh. "I will admit, you were more of a challenge than I expected, but I always knew the bracelet would be mine." Mala kept turning the bracelet over and over in her hands. The bracelet didn't provide much light, but it glowed enough for Litney to see the ecstasy on the creature's face.

Litney felt like she was going to throw up as she wondered what she could have done to have prevented this from happening. She had failed. Failed. There was no stopping her tears. Mala had the bracelet, and that meant Litney had no power to stop her. And Dokken was dead. She curled up into a tiny ball, overcome by all that had happened lately. She thought about how angry she had been at her parents and her life. She remembered the horrible things she had said to her mother. She missed her father. She had lost Dokken. Lost the bracelet to Mala. She had failed.

"What will you do now?" Litney whispered. She knew the answer, but for some reason, she needed to hear it from Mala.

The creature didn't answer.

Litney tried again, "What are you—"

"I'm going to kill you, and then I'm going to take this pretty little bracelet and see how much of this world I can destroy," Mala said without looking up. The creature smiled. "Then I'll move on to another world and do it again and again and again."

Litney put one cheek on the sand; she couldn't stop the tears. But she also couldn't stop watching the bracelet in Mala's hands.

Hands.

Hands. She was supposed to remember something about hands. What was it? She looked at her own hands to see if they would help her remember. No . . . that wasn't it.

Hands and . . . and rain. Something about hands and rain.

Litney looked past Mala to the mouth of the cave and saw that it was raining. She wondered how long the sheets of rain had been pounding the ground. When lightning flashed, Litney was able to make out a tree next to something moving quickly on the ground. Her tears stopped along with her breath as she waited for the lightning to come again. When it did, she squinted and made a discovery—the cave was right next to the river.

Hands and rain. Hands and rain.

She thought back to Grufwin, the dogs, the Rock That Boiled, Trembla. Trembla. No, Litney didn't think the turtle had mentioned anything about hands or rain, but still, that's where her memory stopped and churned. Litney remembered Empira's smile, the wall where she touched the toucan, the library. That was it! The library—the book with the poem in it. But what was the poem? What was it? Litney's mind was frantic.

Hands and rain . . . out you go . . . .

Darnit, Litney couldn't remember. She took a deep breath, closed her eyes, and tried to forget everything that had happened. She put her forehead on the cool sand and imagined herself holding the book in her hands again.

When need is to know
out you go

into the hands of rain where
you will find

a way to make all that is wrong
fade

Great, she had remembered it, but what did it mean? And more importantly, was the poem even talking to her?

She had no idea. Well, that wasn't true. Yes, it was talking to her. She knew it.

The only thing she could really understand was that she needed to get out in the rain. Then maybe she'd know what she was supposed to do.

But how? How was she supposed to get out in the rain? She couldn't sneak past Mala, and even if she did, there were the guards posted outside.

And was she supposed to get Mala to come with her? She didn't know why, but she thought so.

Litney lifted her head. "Can't you kill me afterward?"

"What?" Mala asked.

"I want to see if you can get the bracelet to work. Who knows, maybe it won't work for you. Maybe it only works for the women in my family. Can't you kill me after you try it?" Mala hesitated. In that moment, Litney knew that she had stumbled upon the creature's greatest fear. Plus, Litney guessed that Mala didn't want anyone else to see her fail. Maybe this was the weakness Litney could use to defeat the creature. "That is, unless you are afraid to try."

Mala grabbed Litney by the back of the neck and dragged her outside. The cold rain pelted her skin. *The hands of rain where you will find a way to make all that is wrong fade where you will find a way.* It was hard to think with this rain. It was raining so hard, it felt as if her skin was going to be washed off. Washed off. That was it.

"Fine, you little brat. You want to see me become the most powerful creature ever?"

Mala let her go. Litney watched as Mala put the bracelet on her wrist and then looked at the river. It was only a few feet away from where she and Mala were standing. Before she could calculate how slim her chances of success were, Litney lunged at Mala and sent the two of them tumbling into the water. Cold racing water engulfed them. Litney worked as fast as she could while Mala was still immobile with surprise. She pushed the creature down toward the bottom, praying for something, anything to grab onto. Just as Mala began to recover and struggle, Litney managed to catch onto something. She couldn't believe her luck when she realized it was rope. With four quick circles, Litney wrapped the rope around Mala's neck. The water was dark, but the bracelet on Mala's arm provided just enough light for Litney to see Mala understand what was going on. The creature pointed the bracelet at the girl, but it did nothing except illuminate Litney's determined face. Holding onto the rope, Litney pushed herself off Mala before the creature could grab or stop her. It was dark and her lungs were beginning to burn, but Litney managed to see a big form rushing toward her in the water. Glad she was such a good swimmer, she tucked and did a perfect somersault so her feet met the fallen log first. As she braced her feet against the log, Mala sailed on past, and Litney wrapped the free end of the rope around a branch at her feet again and again and again. The rope tightened until it grew taut and then began shaking. It twisted this way and that. It quivered and shuddered. It went still.

Litney was sure she was going to drown, but she had to see if Mala was dead, and she had to get the bracelet back. She put her hands around the rope and let the water carry her to the end where Mala's body flapped like a flag in the wind.

Mala was dead.

But the bracelet was gone.

* 16 *

Good-Bye

*L*ITNEY HAD TO FIND THE BRACELET. Even though she was cold and exhausted, she spent the next hour or two swimming along the black bottom of the river in the vicinity of Mala's body. The raging river kept carrying her downstream quickly, so she had to keep pulling herself out of the water and walking back along the shore to start all over again.

The last time Litney tried to get out, her hand slipped. After that, there was nothing she could find to grab onto. Bobbing along in the water, she didn't have enough energy left to fight or to be afraid. As the river carried her through the darkness, she thought of Dokken, the bracelet, how miserably she had failed. She started to sob and swallowed so much water she almost drowned. She had to get to shore.

The rain stopped, and finally, the water grew shallow and slowed. Her feet found a sandy bottom, and she waded over to the grassy bank. Grabbing a handful of grass, she pulled herself up and sprawled on the ground. She rolled onto her back and stared at the night sky. A half moon came and went behind clouds.

There were no stars to wish on.

And now there was nothing to stop her from crying.

LITNEY WOKE THE NEXT MORNING to soft fur nuzzling her face. She opened her eyes and squinted because of the bright sun.

Asta.

Litney thought she had used up all of her tears the night before, but apparently not. As the hot wet tears fell down her temples and caught in her hair, Litney sobbed, "I failed."

"Shhh," the bear said, laying down beside Litney.

Litney rolled into the warmth of the bear's massive body, "The bracelet's gone, and, and . . . ." She couldn't go on.

"Dokken?" Asta asked.

Litney nodded.

"We found him when we were looking for you."

Litney turned and buried her face in the bear's fur. Asta said nothing, for the bear knew as well as anyone there was nothing to say.

When Litney's tears subsided, Asta asked, "Why did you do it?"

"I had to," Litney answered. "I couldn't stand to see any more animals hurt. How many?"

Asta shook her head. "We lost many, but not as many as you saved because of your bravery."

"I wasn't brave. I was stupid. If I hadn't—"

"If you hadn't taken on Mala all by yourself, all of us would have died," Asta said.

Suddenly Litney sat up. "Sensho, is Sensho—"

"Sensho's fine. He got a beetle in the eye and will probably never see out of that eye again, but other than that, he's just fine."

"Thank goodness," Litney said, laying back down.

"And some good news is that when all of Mala's creatures discovered she was dead, they fled. And Lando's family wasn't hurt. We found them in another cave right next to—" Asta stopped.

"He was dead when I got there," Litney said. "I don't know what she did to him."

"I had a moose carry him to the Field of Fire. We buried him there," Asta said.

"He would have liked that."

The river gurgled. The clouds floated.

"I don't know what to do now," Litney admitted.

"Go home," Asta said. "Your mother will be anxious to see you."

"But how can I face her? Before I left, I said some terrible things to her. And I've lost the bracelet. I failed."

"Litney, you defeated Mala. You made sure she couldn't harm any more than she already had. You made sure she didn't get the bracelet."

Litney stood and looked at the river. She waded into it and grabbed handfuls of sand and threw them with a scream. She did it again and again until she was covered in water and sand. "I can't go back home," she said when she had fallen to her knees in the river.

"You must," Asta answered from the bank.

"How can I face my mother? And my grandmother? How can I be the Way who lost the bracelet?"

Asta lumbered down the grassy bank and into the water where she stood beside Litney. "You need to say goodbye, and then you have to go back home."

Asta led Litney to a small grove of trees where Sensho was enjoying the attention of a female skunk named Frisia. He had a leaf tied around his eye with a vine.

"I think she likes you," Litney said to Sensho when Frisia and Asta had left them alone.

"You think?"

Litney nodded.

Sensho smiled and touched Litney's hand. "I'm sorry about Dokken. We didn't start off that great, but he was a good kid."

Litney nodded again because she didn't trust her voice.

"I'm going to miss you, Litney of the Bracelet."

"I'm going to miss you, Sensho. Thank you for all you did for me."

"You are most welcome. It was an honor to serve you." Sensho patted her hand again. "Are you going to the Field?"

"I have to."

Sensho lifted Litney's hand and gave it a kiss. "You are amazing. Remember that, will you?"

Litney smiled and stood. She bowed, bowed again, and then left.

Asta and Litney walked along a forest path lined with animals on both sides. As the bear and girl passed, every animal dropped to one knee. Litney opened her mouth to protest, but one look from Asta silenced her. She tried to make sure to look at each animal and nod.

Right before the Field of Fire, a bear stepped in the path and stopped Asta and Litney's progress. "I wanted to say sorry, and to thank you." It was Lando, who was surrounded by his family.

"I was just relieved to hear everyone's okay," Litney said.

One of the little cubs approached her carrying a garland of flowers. Litney knelt down and let the cub put it on her head.

"Thank you," the cub said.

"You're welcome," Litney answered.

"I can't wait to hear the stories they tell about you," the cub said. Litney followed Asta to the edge of the Field of Fire.

"He's over there," Asta whispered.

"Okay," Litney said.

"It's time."

"I know."

"No," Asta said. "It is time for you and me to say goodbye."

"Oh, no. No," Litney said. "I can't."

"Yes," the bear, whose own voice was shaky, replied. "We both know how we began."

"I'm sorr—"

"Shhhh," Asta said. "You must learn when to shush. And I know you are not happy with how this ended, but you have nothing to be ashamed of, my child. You've saved all of us. You've saved me." The bear kissed Litney on the forehead.

"I love you," Litney said.

"I love you. Now go." Asta pushed the girl gently, then turned and ambled off into the forest.

The pile of rocks made it easy to find Dokken's grave. "I don't think I can take any more of this," Litney whispered, but that didn't stop her from making her way toward the place where Dokken's body lay.

When her foot touched one of the rocks, Litney squatted down. "This isn't how this was supposed to end. We were supposed to defeat Mala together, go back home together, and then I would introduce you to my family, and you would convince your parents to move to Minnesota."

Litney reached up and took the crown of flowers from her head. She picked at a purple one. "I lost the bracelet. I tried to find it, but I couldn't. I wanted to save you, but I couldn't do that either." Litney reached out a hand and touched one of the rocks. "I don't know what I would have done without you."

Litney didn't think she'd ever stop crying again. She placed the garland on the rocks. "Goodbye, Dokken. Thanks."

Litney began the long walk back home.

✴ 17 ✴

Home Again

I T TOOK LITNEY ALL DAY to walk back to her grandparents' farm. Most of the time, she followed the river, jumping in several times to swim to the bottom. She was sure the bracelet was calling to her, but each time, she returned to the surface with only fistfuls of mud and muck. When at last she turned to climb the hill where she and Dokken had discovered Trembla's house, Litney stared at the river a long time.

Climbing up out of the river bottom, Litney noticed that Trembla's house was nowhere to be seen. She wasn't surprised. All the magic she had experienced was gone. She wondered what had happened to the backpacks she and Dokken had been given. She couldn't remember when she had used hers last. Not that it mattered. It was just one more thing that she had lost.

At the pond where she and Dokken had met Grufwin, Litney sat down. "I'm tired," she said, but that wasn't the real reason she stopped. She stopped because she wanted to remember the way things were, and she thought maybe the heron could teach her about the way things worked. Not that she hadn't made a fool of herself in front of Grufwin before . . . because she had. She hadn't been able or willing to listen then, but she was now. She was ready to have someone tell her how everything could have gone so wrong, to tell her why Dokken, who had joined her on the adventure by accident, had died.

"Grufwin?"

A frog plopped into the water.

There was no answer.

Litney skipped a rock across the pond's smooth surface and stood up, brushing off the seat of her pants.

The corn in the fields around her seemed to have grown—it reached past her knees. How many days had she been gone? She had no idea. Long enough, but still she stood where she was, just a few minutes from her grandparents. And her mom. She couldn't wait to see them, but she didn't want to have to explain all that had happened. She didn't want to cry. She didn't know if she could bring herself to talk about Dokken. She didn't want to tell them she had lost the bracelet, because she was afraid her mother would give her that look, the same one she had given her daughter when she had found a

six-year-old Litney in the bathroom shaving the cat. Her mother wouldn't even listen as Litney tried to explain. "Mom, your legs are so soft right after you shave them. I wanted to make Kitty feel the same." Her mother had only thrown her that look and then walked away. Litney was sure the same thing was going to happen this time as well.

"But there's no use putting it off."

BERNARD WAS THE FIRST TO SEE HER. He barked and bounded in circles. Litney was almost afraid to call him. "Hey, boy," she said. "Do you want to come here?"

The dog didn't need to be asked twice. He raced toward her and would have knocked her to the ground if she hadn't moved out of his way. She could hardly pet him, he was squirming and whining so much. "Oh, I missed you," she said when she was finally able to bury her face in his neck fur. "Did you miss me?"

Bernard licked her right on the mouth.

"Ugh," she laughed, then straightened when she heard the screen door slam.

"Litney?"

"Hi, Mom."

Lena Way ran to her almost as quickly as the dog had. She scooped her daughter up and twirled her around and around. "Oh, Litney. We've been so worried." Lena pulled back and looked at Litney. "Are you okay? What happened?"

"Can we talk about it later?"

"Oh, well, sure. Yes." Because she didn't know what else to say, Lena asked, "Are you hungry?"

Litney realized she hadn't eaten anything for a very long time. "Yeah, I suppose I am."

Taking her daughter's hand, Lena led Litney up the back steps and into the kitchen. Her grandmother dropped the dough she had been kneading and ran to her, getting flour all over Litney's hair and back.

"Oh, Litney! Litney!" she kept repeating. "We've been so worried."

"I'm sorry," Litney said, because she wasn't sure what else to say.

"Nonsense. There's nothing to be sorry about, honey. We just wanted you home safe and sound." When Lily Way saw that her granddaughter wouldn't look at her, she asked, "Honey, what's wrong?"

Litney's mother intervened. "Mom, she wants something to eat."

"Oh, well, of course," Lily said. "I just made some strawberry bread. I could scramble up some eggs. And some applesauce. And—"

"Just the bread will be fine," Litney said.

"One slice of bread, coming up."

As Lily bustled around the kitchen, Litney sat down in one of the chairs at the small table. Her mother sat opposite her. Litney's grandmother put the plate of bread and butter in front of her with a glass of milk. After Litney had taken several bites, she knew she had to get this over with.

"I failed," she whispered.

"Why don't you start at the beginning and tell us everything," Lena said rubbing a hand on Litney's arm.

"It's hard to explain," Litney said.

"We know," her grandmother responded. "I thought my mother was going to think I was crazy when I sat down to tell her what happened."

"But we've all been through it," Litney's mother said. "It's never quite the same, but we'll understand."

"Well, the first thing is the weirdest. I met a boy in the Atrium, even before the adventure started. He told me he was from New York City." Litney paused to gauge her mother and grandmother's reactions. When they didn't seem surprised by this, her words came gushing out like the river she had spent so much time beside. She told them everything, from her rudeness to Grufwin to the first meeting with Mala. She described the magic of Trembla's house and how they had come to meet Sensho. And Asta. The words grew more difficult as she neared the end of her story, but she somehow managed to tell them about Dokken and losing the bracelet.

"I failed," she repeated when the story had ended. Her eyes dropped to her hands. "I'm sorry." Litney looked up at her mother and her grandmother as a painful realization hit her. "And, and now my daughter won't be able to . . . to . . ." she began to weep.

Lena knelt beside Litney's chair, and Litney collapsed into her mother's arms. "Shhhh, sweetie. Shhhh. It's okay. Oh, Litney, my brave, brave girl." Even though every part of her wanted to argue, Lena knew what Litney needed most right now was to cry and to be held while she cried.

It was hard to say how long the storm of Litney's tears lasted, but when they were gone, the three women knew they had shared something none of them would forget.

"Now," said Lena. "About this failing."

"Mom," Litney began.

Lena put a finger to her lips. "Shhhh," she said. "You need to know when to shush."

Litney laughed so hard, a bunch of wet stuff came out of her nose. "Sorry. Asta said the same thing."

"Then I'm doubly grateful to her—for protecting you and for telling you things in my stead. Litney, you obviously had a very different experience than your grandmother or I did. But I want you to know how proud we are of you. From what you told us, you were nothing but courageous and kind."

"Litney," her grandmother said, "have you heard the saying 'Sometimes you have to lose the battle to win the war'?"

"Yes." Litney could tell her grandmother wanted her to explain what it meant. "It means sometimes in order to overcome, you have to lose along the way."

"Exactly," Lily said with a satisfied nod. "You defeated Mala, and it sounds like that was the war. So, you lost the bracelet. I think the bracelet would have rather been lost than for you not to defeat Mala. Like your mother said, we're proud of you. You did exactly what you needed to do."

Litney thought about this for a moment. She shrugged. "I don't know."

Her mother hugged her. "We're so glad you're okay. Pop has been worried sick about you."

"Where is he?"

"He went to town to pick up some things, but he'll be back by suppertime," her grandmother answered.

"Litney," her mother said, running a hand through her daughter's curling hair, "maybe you should go to the Atrium. I know how much you love it there, and after all that's happened, you might, I don't know, find some peace there."

Litney surprised her mother by nodding. "I think I will. Thanks, Mom." She gave her mom a hug, then her grandma. She whistled to Bernard and went out the back door, calling over her shoulder, "I'll be back by dinner."

As they watched Litney walk away, Lena put an arm around her mother. "That was one of the hardest things I have ever had to do," she said.

"I know, dear. I know."

"I couldn't bear to tell her that we all lose the bracelet at the end," Lena said.

"Or that we all meet a boy."

The two women giggled.

BERNARD WASN'T ABOUT TO LET LITNEY out of his sight. He followed right on her heels as she ducked into the Atrium.

"No panting," Litney warned.

The dog panted.

"Oh, you," she said, scratching his thick neck. Litney sat down cross legged on the ground and listened to the birds. She didn't hear any of them talking this time, but their songs began to calm her. She lay back and put her head on the ground. The ivy looked the same, the roses smelled the same. Litney closed her eyes.

She didn't know how long she had slept when something woke her. A noise near her feet. Litney stretched as she sat up.

A box.

No, *the* box. The same box she had found at the garage sale. Like a ball rolling down a hill, her heart quickly picked up speed. "It can't be," she whispered. "Can it?"

She crawled over to the box as if it were an animal she was trying not to scare away. When she touched it, it felt different than it had before—it wasn't warm and soft. It was like cool silk.

"Oh, please," she whispered.

She opened the box and the bracelet was inside. Litney couldn't stop the smile, the joy, and she didn't even ask how. "Oh my, oh, oh I'm glad you're safe," she said. The stone glowed at her.

She put the bracelet on but it didn't feel right and warm on her wrist as it had before. "Maybe I'm not supposed to wear it anymore," Litney said. With one last caress, Litney took it off her wrist and put it back in the box. After she had closed the lid, Litney picked the box up, meaning to carry it back to the farmhouse. She had to show her mom and grandma. As soon as she got to the door of the Atrium, however, the wood became so hot that she dropped the box. "Ouch!" she cried. She picked the bracelet up from the dirt, brushed it off and put it back in the box to try again. When the same thing happened, Litney looked around and saw a piece of paper and a pen lying over where the box had been.

It took her a minute. "Oh." Her stomach went heavy and light, all at the same time. "The note. For my daughter."

"MOM? GRANDMA?" LITNEY CALLED WHEN she came in the screen door. She couldn't wait to tell them about the bracelet.

"We're in the dining room, dear," her grandmother said.

The clock on the wall told Litney she had just made it in time for dinner. She pushed through the swinging door and then screamed.

"Daddy!"

Epilogue

*L*ITNEY WAS TRYING TO FINISH HER MATH homework before the eight o'clock bell and before her teacher noticed. She hadn't had time to finish it the night before because she and her parents had gone on a picnic and hadn't gotten home until late.

Her parents were around a lot more lately. After they had driven home from her grandparents, the three of them had sat at the kitchen table and talked. That night her parents had promised to travel less and spend more time together as a family. Luckily, a few weeks ago Litney's parents had gotten a huge grant from some foundation so they could hire others to do much of their work for them. Life wasn't perfect, but it was better.

"Litney," her teacher, Mrs. Swenson, said. "I've got a note here that you need to go to the office."

"But—"

"You can finish your homework later," Mrs. Swenson said with a twinkle in her eye.

"How did you know? Oh, never mind. See you." The girl gave her teacher a little wave and skittered out of the room. In the hall, she said hello to a couple of her friends, then fought her way down the hall against all the bodies who seemed to be going in the opposite direction than she was.

"What's up?" she asked Miss Louise who worked in the main office.

"We've got a new student we'd like you to show around for the day."

"Okay. Where?"

Miss Louise pointed to a boy sitting in a chair behind her.

"Dokken? Oh, my gosh! Dokken!" Litney ran over and hugged him.

The boy pushed her away. "Who are you and how do you know my name?"

"Dokken, it's me, Litney. Don't you remember?"

"Remember what? My family just moved here."

"From New York City?" Litney asked, smug.

Dokken looked at Miss Louise. "She's kind of freaking me out. Do I have to go around with her?"

"Litney? How do you know all this?" Miss Louise asked, her round face quite concerned.

It was then that Litney understood. Well, she didn't understand exactly, but that was okay. "I'm sorry. I must have heard some kids talking about you," she said.

"But—" Miss Louise said.

"Come on," Litney said, taking the paper from Miss Louise's hand that had Dokken's schedule and locker number on it.

Dokken hesitated but for only a second. After all, this was the first person he had ever met in his whole life who hadn't made fun of his name.

* Preview *

Chapter One
of
* The Fountain *

BUT HOW?" DOKKEN CARVER ASKED over his shoulder as Litney Way followed him through the weeds. Litney had just finished telling him about everything that had happened with the bracelet—from the magic backpacks to how she'd been able to fly. The two of them were heading toward a copse of birch trees in the wetlands that took up acres and acres of land behind Dokken's new house. His parents had moved to Minnesota in the fall, coming from New York City, the land of steel and glass to settle in a town without even one stoplight. It wasn't that Dokken didn't like it here. He just couldn't get over the land— how it went on and was everywhere. Dokken took a moment to absorb all Litney had told him, and then he went on to pronounce, "No way."

"That's what I thought," Litney replied with a shrug. "When I first got the bracelet, I was pretty mean to my mom. I kept demanding that she tell me what was going on because it was all so bizarre, but she couldn't. She said I had to find out for myself. Then I went out into the Atrium on my grandparents' farm. You came in right after I heard the birds talking, and . . ." Here Litney grinned. "Then off we went."

"Uh huh."

"You were in totally rumpled clothes, wearing only one sock." Litney looked at the red-headed Dokken ahead of her as they trekked through the weeds and smiled. "Kind of like now."

He cut her a scowl. "Very funny. But I died," Dokken came back to this detail for the third time, turning to look at Litney with his amazingly blue eyes.

"Yes."

"But I'm not dead," he insisted.

Dokken turned forward again and kept walking. "And I don't remember dying. You'd think if you died, you'd remember it." He liked Litney. He really did. She was the best friend he'd ever had. The only friend he'd really ever had. But she was crazy. How in the world had he magically appeared in Minnesota even though he'd been asleep in his bed in New York? How could he have gone to a different world or dimension or whatever where animals talked? How could he have read Litney's mind and how could she, a girl, fly? And this bracelet. It magically appears, it magically disappears. That didn't make any sense at all. But even if all that was true, and he was sure it wasn't, there was no way he could have died. That kept hitting him like that big old meat cleaver his mother used to tenderize chicken. And then somehow, miraculously his parents had up and decided to move to Minnesota, and he ended up in the same school as Litney . . . and this had happened after he had died, even though he was now *not* dead. It was crazy, and thinking about this whole thing gave him the willies.

"That's why I was so thrilled to see you when I stepped into the principal's office because it meant you weren't really dead," Litney explained as if that solved the whole thing. She undid the binder holding her shoulder-length curly brown hair and put it up again. It was getting warm; she wanted all the hair off her neck.

"I thought you were crazy when you screamed my name," Dokken admitted.

"And what do you think of me now that I've told you all this?" Litney tried to keep her voice light, teasing, but she didn't succeed. When Dokken didn't answer right away, she rushed on, "I know, I shouldn't have told you all this. I should have waited. Or never said anything. Ever." Litney couldn't say why she had chosen that day to tell Dokken all of this. The two of them had gotten to know each other throughout the past school year, and now that it was summer break, they were spending all their time together. Still, she hadn't even known him a year, and when she had thought time and again about telling him all of this, she had decided she would never tell him about their adventure together. She was too glad to have him as a friend. She didn't want to risk losing that. But for some reason, as they walked across this countryside today, she had felt her mouth open and the story come pouring out, almost like pop squirting from a bottle that had been shaken up. There was no stopping it, no holding it back. "Look, I don't blame you if you don't believe me. And I sure don't blame you if you don't want to, you know, be my friend anymore."

"No," Dokken said, then hesitated. He wanted to make her feel better by adding, "I'm glad you told me," but he couldn't. He'd be lying if he said that, so he said, "But you don't have the bracelet anymore?"

"No, once I got back, I had to write a note to my future daughter and then I had to put it back in the box." Litney's dark-brown eyes grew troubled. "Besides thinking you were dead, giving up the bracelet was the hardest thing I've ever had to face."

"Do you think you'll ever get to see it again? Like when you turn sixteen? That's when your mom and grandma received it, right?"

"Yes, but somehow I doubt it. I think I've had my chance."

"Do you want it back again?" Dokken asked as he slapped his neck, then scratched the spot to get rid of the carcass of whatever bug had just bitten him.

"I don't know," Litney replied honestly. "It was scary when I had it. I really didn't know if I could survive any of it or make any difference."

She closed her eyes and even though the sun was warm on her face, she shivered. She shivered as she remembered the dogs that had attacked them, the way Mala had pulled her under the water, the quiet and fear as she had waited for Mala's forces to attack. But then she remembered the delight of flying and the Song of Silence and the crushing loving hug of Asta the bear. The fear receded. She repeated, "I don't know."

The two of them had reached the birch trees. They had never ventured this far out into the wetlands before, but they had packed a lunch. That meant they could be out in the countryside for the whole day. "What's that?" Litney asked, pointing through the trees to a space ahead of them.

"It's hard to tell," Dokken answered, squinting. "Some sort of old building, maybe."

"And look, there are more buildings over there. I'll bet it's an old abandoned farm place."

"Wanna explore?" Dokken asked, a smile widening his lips.

Litney returned the smile. "Sure."

* *

Acknowledgments

This book would not have been possible without Corinne and Seal Dwyer at North Star Press. I am glad not only for their editorial insights but for their willingness to get this book off my computer's hard drive and out into the real world.

It was a true delight to work with Mary Bruno on the cover and artwork and to have her take the characters out of my head and give them a real form. More of her work can be seen at her website at www.mcb-press.com.

I would like to thank Kane Klick, Jonathan Hawkins, Robert Hawkins, Katherine Dickinson, and Keith Spears for reading the manuscript at its various stages and giving me great insights and suggestions.

How many times I would have stopped writing altogether if it weren't for Len Edgerly, Kim Hunter-Perkins, and Olga Abella. Thank you for being constant sources of calm and encouragement.

Besides dedicating this to my own kids, I also want to dedicate it to my nieces and nephew: Michaela Flippin, Alex Flippin, Maisy Miller,

Hannah Johnson, Laura Johnson, Anna Johnson and Andrew Johnson. May your lives be filled with adventures—the good kind.

Thank you to my mother, Jeannine Johnson, and my in-laws, Laban and Sylvia Miller. Dad, I wish you had been here to see this.

Finally, Shane, Ben and Elise. Your support and joy in this process has been a gift I will cherish forever.